Frances Fairweather

NOV 09

D0610485

by the same author
HARD CASH
THE GOOD WOLF
THE MAGICAL WORLD OF LUCY-ANNE

DEREK SMITH

Frances Fairweather – Demon Striker!

ff

faber and faber

First published in Great Britain in 1996
Published in this paperback edition in 2000
by Faber and Faber Limited
3 Queen Square London WC1N 3AU

Photoset by Avon Dataset, Bidford on Avon
Printed in England by Mackays of Chatham plc, Chatham, Kent

© Derek Smith, 1996

The right of Derek Smith to be identified as author of this
work has been asserted in accordance with Section 77
of the Copyright, Designs and Patents Act 1988

A CIP record for this book
is available from the British Library

ISBN 0–571–20655–7

2 4 6 8 10 9 7 5 3 1

To Rebecca,
who also enjoys a kick-about
over Wanstead Flats

I

My teacher says there is more to life than football. But I think she has to say that. It's her job. I mean she's not a football coach – is she?

My best friend, Anne, agrees with me. Football is it! It's first, second, third . . . all the way up to ten, and *maybe* then comes music. Or maybe then comes football again.

You have guessed by now that I am crazy about football. I got it off my dad; he's plain crazy. Right now he's growing a giant marrow. He says he wants it to fill a wheelbarrow. I think that is crazy, I can't stand marrow, and a wheelbarrow-full . . . Yuk!

My friend, Anne, started a girls' football team at school, which is great. The trouble is we can't get any matches, which is lousy. We won both the last two and I scored four goals.

I get near a goal and something takes over. I know where to be, I know exactly where the goal is without looking. I know which foot to shoot with, and when a header is the thing. I can sense where the goalie is. It just happens when I'm near a goal. Like magnetism.

Today Anne and I are going to have a kick-about. I'd rather have a match any day but when you can't get the matches – you have to take second best. Not that Anne is second best. No way, no way. She is the only one who understands the way I feel.

Ms Natches is in charge of the team, though we set it up. Me and Anne suggested it, and we got enough girls for it.

Ms Natches runs the training sessions and organizes the matches. I wonder sometimes if she's trying that hard. I mean she's my class teacher, and she's the one that said there's more to life than football. Now if she really thinks that, maybe she thinks there's more to life than organizing football matches.

Me and Anne want to get a team in the girls' league, so then it's nothing to do with school. Then Ms Natches can't say, 'No training for you unless you finish that history.' Or geography or science – or maths. Like she does.

She doesn't realize that none of those things are important.

I find Anne over Wanstead Flats, by the changing rooms. We don't use them; we come over in our tracksuits. The wall, though, is good for a goal when there's just two of you.

It's drizzling, which is fine by us as it clears away the people, especially mickey-taking boys, who always want to challenge you to a match. The last couple of weeks there have been a lot of them around throwing bits of wood up into the conker trees, which edge one end of the flats. Under the trees are masses of broken conker cases and twigs and, occasionally, a conker they have missed. I always pick them up. My dad likes them.

The Flats are big and flat, which you would expect. Mostly grass but with a few patches of trees crowded together, and looking lonely today in the mist. There are cows on it, so you get a few cow-pats. But then it's worth it to see the cows, usually black-and-white ones.

When we train together Anne and me have a sort of routine. We practise passing for a while, then shooting (with both feet), and then dribbling round tent-pegs. Anne has a stopwatch and we time this, going in and out the pegs, round the tree, back in and out the pegs, then shooting.

It's a killer. Like getting a pass in your own half, taking it right down the pitch and shooting. Sometimes I can score when we do it, though Anne is a good goalie – in fact she fills in when our regular goalie, Maisie, can't make it. Other times I'm so beat when I get to the end that I can hardly kick the ball, and Anne virtually takes it off my toe.

But then football is a team game, and you'd have to be crazy to go all the way up the pitch without passing. Or else, Superman.

Anyway we're both zonked after half an hour, and we sit on a bench under a tree. I have some water in my bag and a few biscuits. Anne has some sweets. We place them between us and share.

'So when's our next match, Anne?'

She shrugs. 'Ms Natches says she's trying.'

I sniff. 'She always says that.'

Anne imitates her voice. It's sort of posh, with her voice up in her nose somewhere. 'It's difficult, darling. There aren't many girls' teams in schools, you know?'

'So what's new, Hatchback?'

'If there aren't the teams, dearest – I can't get the matches, darling.'

All that 'dearest, darling' stuff – I poke my tongue out.

'Don't you poke your tongue out at me, Frances Fairweather,' says Anne, looking very severe, 'or I'll have your father in.'

I groan. 'Oh don't remind me. She's having him over tomorrow after school . . .' I did not want to think about it. This was his second visit. It was going to be heavy.

'What's it about?' asks Anne.

'Oh the usual,' I say.

We both knew what that is. There's no need to say any

3

more. I break the last biscuit in two, and give her one bit.

'You know in Italy,' she says, 'they have women's professional football?'

'Then let's tell Hatchback to get us a game in Italy!' I jump up. I'm suddenly feeling in a fever. I run about, heading, kicking, passing. The Italian crowd are roaring. I take a pass off the centre line, burst into their half. Beat one defender, nutmeg the next. Then as two more come – I cross the ball to our left winger. She takes it, and I pull away from my marker . . . and into the gap as the ball comes across the area . . . and crack it into the net!

'Goal!' I yell.

'I'll run out on the field with my autograph book . . .' exclaims Anne.

I throw my arms high and clap them over my head. 'Franc-es! Franc-es! We want Franc-es!'

Anne holds an imaginary microphone in front of her. 'Tottenham Hotspur have offered a million for Frances Fairweather . . .'

I wave it away. 'Peanuts.'

'Liverpool are offering two million . . .'

I hold my head snootily in the air. 'Tell 'em I'll talk it over with my agent.'

'Real Madrid say name your price . . .'

I am supercool. 'Big money, big big money . . . We're talking billions, baby.'

Anne takes a cigar out of her mouth and grabs my hand. 'It's a deal, honey.'

'Dust my shoelace, scum.'

'Yes ma'am, no ma'am . . . three bags full ma'am . . .'

'And that reporter from the *Sun*. How long's he been waiting now?'

'Three hours, your Highness.'

4

'Keep him waiting another three . . . then tell him I'm busy.'

We both roll up laughing. The dream is over. I wonder sometimes if it is a dream, and how I would be if it came to it. I mean I know I'm good. Would I really be such a pig if I did make it big?

'You got the style, Frances Fairweather,' says Anne. 'You can sure put on an act.'

'You're not so bad, Anne Harper.'

Anne sniffs. 'Then how come *I* never get to play the superstar.'

I think for a second. 'Maybe it's because I'm no good at small parts.'

Anne throws her bag at me.

School is boring.

It wasn't so bad when Natches let me sit next to Anne. But then she decided that we weren't doing any work, and she moved me. Even though I have promised many times that I will really work, really hard, if only she'd let me sit next to Anne again, she still said no and won't discuss it again. Which you must admit is pretty mean.

You see what I mean about Hatchback?

Our class is a big box with windows out in the playground. There's five of them altogether, raised up so you can crawl underneath, if you *like* crawling around in dust and rubbish. Being out in the playground is good at playtime because you can get straight out, and then play football to the very last minute. It's bad in the summer, when you just fry. Even with all the windows open we're all dying. At long last they've put blinds in, but we don't need them now it's autumn.

That's typical of our school.

I have to sit next to Joe. Joe is a swot, and the idea is that this will rub off on me. Well, I have decided it won't. But the problem is it does a bit. Because sometimes school is so boring, there is just nothing else to do. I mean, when Joe is beavering away – and Anne is way over the other side of the class – what else can I do but work some of the time?

Joe is on Book 5 mathematics. I am on Book 2. He works so quickly that he gives me earache turning the pages. But then he's finished, and he tries to help me. The best thing to do, I've found, is to act stupid. That way Joe gets exasperated and does my work for me.

'Don't you understand what I am saying?' he says. And I shake my head, because I haven't been listening. Then he shows me how to do it, and invites me to do the next one. And when I do it wrong, he shows me how to do it, and so on. I've got him to do a whole page that way.

This term we are doing the Tudors. I got a bit interested in them when I found out they played football, but when I found out that the teams could be two whole villages – I thought, I don't think much of the Tudors. And if Henry the Sixth had eight wives, or was it the Seventh had nine wives – all I can say is I am glad I wasn't one of them.

We were supposed to be drawing a Tudor house this lesson. You draw the outside first, then put it on a second sheet of paper, cut round the house, then on the bottom sheet draw what's in the house. And if you've finished that you can write about what the family would be doing. Yawn.

And that's where Joe's got to. Not yawning, but he's finished the house. It's beautifully coloured, and he's cut round it and put chairs and cupboards inside. He's even drawn people. It's not yet afternoon play, and he's written three-quarters of a page on what the family are doing. I look over his shoulder.

'Do your own work, Frances,' calls out Hatchback.

I get back to my own work, but it's not what she thinks it is. I am drawing Amy Friday, as she was in *Women's Football*. There's two defenders coming for her, and she's jumping high between them to head the ball. I am drawing it carefully so no one can tell what I am doing. I have got a large sheet of paper, but I have folded it up so it's a thin strip, and I am drawing a bit at a time, then unfolding the next piece. When I get home I will iron out the creases.

7

'What you up to?' whispers Joe.

'None of your business,' I say, putting my arm round it. 'Get on with your own work.'

'I've finished,' he says.

You would, I think. He's annoying me now, because he won't give up. He knows I am not doing what I should.

'Go away,' I say. 'Shove off.'

He pulls at my arm. 'That's not history.'

'You do your thing, I'll do mine.' And I give him a big push. Joe falls out of his chair, and the class laughs as he picks himself up.

'What's going on over there?' says Teacher.

'I just fell over,' mumbles Joe.

'I think you were pushed,' says Hatchback, and uh-oh she's coming across.

Now she's standing over me, hands on hips, and I know I've had it. I used to think she was pretty, but I have definitely changed my mind these last few weeks. She's got a thin moustache over her top lip, which curls when she calls you out. She ties her hair in a pony-tail, and it isn't natural. If you look close you can see the roots coming through. What I really don't like is when she tears up your work in front of you. It makes you feel like a beetle she's going to crunch underfoot.

'Have you finished your Tudor house, Frances?'

'Nearly, Ms.' I have my arm right round it, and I can feel her eyes burning into my neck.

'Always *nearly*,' says Ms Natches. 'The day you say I've finished, Ms – I shall die of shock.'

'Won't be long, Ms,' I say in a weak voice.

She tries to draw my arms away. 'Show me what you've done, my dear.'

'Can't I finish it first?' I am holding on tight.

'Show me it now, Frances.' Her voice is soft and determined. I don't know why I just don't give in. Yes, I do. I'm going to get done, and I'm trying to avoid it for as long as possible.

'I've only a bit to do, Ms Natches.'

'The more you go on, dearest – the more suspicious I become.'

She jerks the paper. It tears, and I curse inside – it was a really good picture of Amy Friday. Hatchback has got enough to know it isn't a Tudor house. It's more like a pair of legs with football boots on the end.

She says, 'I see.' Her face is icy, mouth small, breathing heavily.

'I was going to do my Tudor house when I finished this picture,' I tried.

Teacher shook her head and sighed. 'No, when you finished that one, lovey, you'd simply do another one.'

I make myself small, and try something different. 'I'm no good at history, Ms.'

By now the whole class has stopped. They are really enjoying this.

'And how would you know that, Frances?' She is looking at me as if to burn my eyes out. 'You never *do* any history. You're absolutely obsessed by football.'

'That's what my dad says.'

'Well, he is absolutely right.'

Keep her talking, I think to myself. She might weaken like Mum does, and I won't get it quite so bad.

'What's wrong with being obsessed by football, Ms Natches?'

'It isn't the only thing in the world, dear.'

'It is for me.'

'But it's only a game.'

9

How many times have I heard that! From my Mum, my Aunt Harriet, my Uncle Bill, half the world . . . .

I say, 'Ms, some people are crazy about pop stars, some about TV stars, some about fashion and computer games. Me – I just love football.'

Teacher takes a few steps away from me. She is talking to me, but she is also talking to the class. She wants to get them on her side.

'I don't mind you loving football, Frances – up to a point. And that point is when it affects your schoolwork. Fine – support your local team, play it, follow it . . . but *live* for football? Think about nothing else? You've reached the point where football ceases to be a game. It becomes a sickness. You are an addict.'

'Better football than drugs,' I mumble.

She sighs. 'If only you didn't have a smart reply every time.' She flaps her hands at me. 'You're a bright girl, Frances, but your schoolwork is terrible. It's true you are not very good at history . . . but if you don't do any, that's not surprising. Nor will you be any good at geography, maths or science . . . if the only thing in your head is football, football, football.' She stops, and holds up the half-picture of a footballer.

The class laughs. Even Anne can't hold it in.

Teacher swings around to the class. 'Anyone who thinks it funny will stay in at playtime with Frances.'

The laughter stops, but there are a lot of smirks being held in tightly.

'I am seeing your father this evening, Frances. I have had just about enough.'

'Of what, Ms?' I ask innocently.

She walks back to me, and puts her head close to mine, until she is staring in my eyes from a few centimetres away.

'Of football, Frances. Of football.'

I can't take the stare. I look down at the table, and can feel her breath on me as she speaks.

'Between me and your parents, we are going to cure you, Frances Fairweather. I promise you that.'

3

I had wanted to go off with Anne and have a kick-about after school, but that was out. Hatchback had set me some maths. 'Catching up,' she called it. I called it a liberty.

Dad walked nervously into the classroom, fingering his cap.

'I've er . . . put my cab in the school car park? Is that all right?'

'Well, it's only for staff . . .' said Ms Natches.

'You want me to move it then?' I could tell he was more scared of Hatchback than I was.

'Leave it for now,' she said.

Dad nodded. 'Right.'

'But in future . . .'

Dad nodded again like a polly-parrot. 'In future. Don't worry, in future – I'll know.' He stopped, out of breath, though why that should be I don't know. My dad keeps fit. He goes for a run every morning, plays football Sunday mornings, works on the allotment two or three times a week, not to mention his weight training which he does in our cellar.

'About Frances,' began Teacher. 'You know the problem, I'm sure.'

Dad nodded again. 'Football.'

Ms Natches gave a deep sigh. 'I like football. I run the girls' team . . . but there have to be limits.'

Dad was nodding again, rolling his cap around in his hands. 'Oh yes, got to be limits.'

'Let me be frank, Mr Fairweather,' said Ms Natches. 'It's nothing but football from the minute your daughter comes in the class to the minute she leaves.'

Dad nodded again. I wished he'd stop it. It looked silly. They weren't paying any attention to me so I'd stopped doing maths.

Ms Natches went on, 'She doesn't listen. When she's not drawing footballers, she's got this dreamy far-away look . . . as if she's the key-striker for England in a breakaway. Where does she get it from?'

Dad looked as if he'd been accused of bank robbery. He was shifting his cap round and round like a steering wheel. 'It's my fault,' he said.

'Ah,' said Ms Natches, like a spider beckoning a fly on.

Dad was so nervous now he was making me sweat. 'To tell you the truth, I wanted a son . . .'

'Ah,' said Ms Natches.

'I've always been keen on sports, and I wanted to teach my son boxing. The noble art. Three three-minute rounds! I was London champion myself. Well, when Frances was born . . . my first reaction was disappointment. What do you do with . . . a girl? Then I thought, *Why not? I'll teach her to box.* So I got her on road work, skipping, punch-bag . . .'

It was Teacher's turn to nod. 'How old was she?'

'Three,' said Dad.

Ms Natches' eyes opened wide. 'You were teaching a three-year-old to box?'

Dad gave her a weak smile. 'Start 'em young, that's my motto. The problem was, her mum had a thing or two to say . . .'

'That doesn't surprise me.'

Dad sighed. 'In fact her mother decided boxing was out. So I turned to my second love. Football. Every week I'd take her up West Ham or Leyton Orient, depending who was playing at home. When she was really little I'd have her up on my shoulders to see over the crowd. She had her rattle and horn. Up the 'Ammers! Up the Orient! Then in the garden I set up a dozen gnomes for her to dribble round, two beanpoles for goals . . . We'd finish with circuit training, sprinting and a penalty shoot-out, so by the time she was five . . .'

'Five!' exclaimed Hatchback.

'. . . I'd taught her all I knew,' Dad went on. 'And I had to go on an advanced coaching course to stay ahead. So don't blame the girl, Ms Matches.'

'Natches.'

'Er, Natches. You see – I brought her up wrong. *My* obsession led to her obsession. Don't blame the girl.'

The two of them were walking round me like I was a hole in the ground. I was beginning to get angry. I did exist. *I* had rights too.

Teacher rubbed her chin thoughtfully. 'So that's how it came about. But what do we do? She's a bright girl, your daughter. There's so much there. But it's all smothered in football. I don't know what will happen when she gets to secondary school.'

'She'll bunk off,' said Dad.

'And what will that lead to?' asked Ms Natches, with raised eyebrows.

Dad was looking at his cap, shaking his head. 'I did a bit of bunking off myself. And I must say that some of the things we did . . .' He sucked in a breath. 'I don't want her going that way.'

'Then we must break Frances' obsession with football,' Teacher said quietly.

Dad sighed. 'Yes.'

'Why?' I burst in.

Ms Natches had sat down on my table, tapping it with her forefinger. 'She plays for my girls' team.'

'Yes,' said Dad. 'The Perils they call themselves – don't they?'

Teacher stood up. 'Time we stopped her.'

'What!' I yelled. I turned to Dad. 'Dad, she can't . . .'

Dad waved me down. 'Keep out of this, love.' He turned back to Teacher. 'It seems a bit cruel. I know what you are saying, but I mean . . .'

'I wouldn't normally suggest it, but the way it is now, she might as well leave school for all she's doing here. Her future depends on her realizing that football isn't all there is to life.'

Dad was chewing a thumbnail. *Come on, Dad*, I was thinking. *Stop her. Tell her what's what.*

'All right,' he said, nodding. 'We'll stop her playing for the girls' team.'

I hit the table. 'You can't *do* this to me!'

'Stay out of this, Frances.'

'Dad!'

'Leave it to me.'

'But, Dad . . .'

'I said leave it to me.'

I sank into a chair.

Ms Natches was smiling. She had picked up Dad's nod. 'I'm glad we've had this chat, Mr Fairweather,' she said. 'A little firmness now, and in a few weeks Frances will realize this has all been for her own good.' She looked at her watch. 'Goodness. I've got a staff meeting. Please excuse me, Mr Fairweather.'

'Certainly,' said Dad. 'I appreciate your concern, Ms Natches. Come on, girl. Your teacher's got more to do than complain about you.'

In the playground, as we made our way to the car park, I said, 'You can't, Dad. You can't stop me playing for the Perils.'

Dad had his arm round my shoulder. 'I'm sorry, love. But there has to be a bit less football in your life.'

I shrugged his arm off. 'It's not fair.'

He stopped me, and turned me towards him, a finger under my chin. 'You'll just have to improve your schoolwork – then, all right, you can play. But in the meantime . . .'

'I'm suspended.' I closed my eyes, and felt the world spinning away from me.

'You can kick about, Frances – but there's to be no matches with the girls. And I'm stopping your football magazines. You get me?'

I got him. I could kick the wall, kick trees, kick myself – but I couldn't kick a football into a goal.

4

Dad dropped me off in the cab after school, and then went off to work. I had sat in the back, not saying another word to him.

We've got a small front yard with a tired-looking rose in it and some pots of summer plants which Dad keeps saying he's going to clear out and put some bulbs in.

Most of the houses are joined together and face another lot, more or less the same. Nearly all of them have two floors built in dirty yellow brick. They have dates on like 1887. Mum and Dad say ours is falling to bits. Every so often they do some repairs but the house always catches up. They want to modernize it, but say they just can't afford it.

So that's where I live. But don't think just because the street is old that it's run down. It's just not posh.

Ordinary, I suppose.

I went in to see Mum. *I'll get her on my side*, I thought. *She can twist Dad round, and Hatchback can go hang herself.* And, the way I felt, I'd gladly give her the rope.

Mum was in the kitchen, which was covered in wood shavings. Mum makes dolls' houses. She takes orders, mostly from friends, but sometimes complete strangers will ring her up. She doesn't advertise, though. Word just gets about.

She works in the kitchen, which I've got used to. A bit of sawdust in my packed lunch adds to the flavour. It's the glue I can't stand.

'They've stopped me playing football,' I said.

There was a dolls' house on the table, and she was putting

17

tiny hinges on the front door. She had a streak of red paint on her forehead.

'I know,' she said.

I looked at her in amazement. I'd only just got in. How could she?

'Your Dad and I talked it over last night.'

'Talked what over?'

Mum put down her small screwdriver. 'When we got the letter from your teacher asking us to come in to see her, we knew what it was about.'

I kicked the table.

'Stop that!' shouted Mum. 'I've just glued the sides.'

'Sorry,' I mumbled, though I wanted to push the whole thing off.

'A bit less football won't do you any harm, Frances.' She paused, looking at me sadly. 'Do you want to give me a hand?'

'No,' I said, walking out the back door.

'I've been grounded,' I said to Anne.

'I know,' said Anne kicking the ball against the wall.

'How did you know?' I exclaimed.

'Your dad saw me and explained,' she said, keeping the ball moving.

I didn't join her as I normally would have done, but sat with my head on my chin. We were over Wanstead Flats in our usual place. The day was overcast with silver grey clouds which seemed to join up with the grass in a distant mist.

'Everyone seems to know about me.'

Anne stopped kicking. 'I am sorry,' she said. She sat down by me, and put her arm round my shoulder. 'I think they're mean.'

'I can't play for the Perils,' I moaned.

'They're stupid,' said Anne. 'You're our best player. And I bet it won't make any difference to your schoolwork.'

I looked at Anne. I wasn't sure what she meant by that. Was she saying I was stupid? That I couldn't work if I wanted to? Oh, who cared! I lay back on the grass and kicked my legs.

'I tried to tell your Dad,' said Anne.

'Thanks,' I said.

'I said it's your life. I said you're taking away the only thing she cares about . . .'

'Oh Anne . . .' I wanted to cry.

'He said it's for your own good.'

I got up and punched the air. 'They *always* say that! Whenever they do something that hurts, they tell you it's for your own good.'

'I told him it wasn't fair.'

'How would he feel if I took his marrow away, or if I told Mum she couldn't make dolls' houses. "It's for your own good," I would say. "Oh yes – this hurts me more than it hurts you." ' I slammed the ball into the wall. 'I hate them all! Every single pokey one of them!'

'I'm going to get a petition up from the girls in the team.'

'At least *you're* standing by me,' I said.

'You're my best friend,' said Anne.

I kicked the ball to her. She passed it back. I threw it in the air. She headed it over. I headed it back. She trapped it, and passed.

'At least,' I said, 'the Perils haven't got any matches for a while.'

'Yes, they have,' said Anne.

I stopped the ball. 'Who with?'

'St Mary's. Thursday evening.'

I went wild. I stomped about, treading on every grown-up I knew. I jumped up and down on them. I pummelled them into the earth. I was a sledgehammer of anger.

'That settles it!' I exclaimed.

'What?'

'The Perils aren't the only team.'

'They're the only *girls'* team around here.'

'So?' I said.

Anne caught my eye. 'Are you thinking what I think you are thinking?' she said.

I gave her a wicked grin. 'Yes.'

5

Half an hour later we were at the Tigers' football ground.

It doesn't belong to the Tigers. Their ground is a public playing-field where they have their hut, and where they train and play their matches.

It's all grass, apart from a bit of it which is fenced off, with high tennis court fencing. That has a red grit surface and a couple of floodlights for winter training.

The hut is about ten metres back from the pitch. If you continued the centre line you'd get to it. It's really just a large garden shed: a window, a door, a roof and dark-brown wooden panels. A kid's idea of a house.

As we came into the field we could see they were having a practice match, six-a-side. All the players wore the club colours; orange-and-black striped shirts and orange shorts. One team wore green sashes as well, to distinguish them. Running up and down the pitch was the coach, shouting orders. We had heard him from the street. He wanted them to do long passes. He was shouting non-stop, getting very angry, his arms waving like a helicopter rotor.

Anne looked at me. 'This team?'

I looked back at the man on the boil. That was Stan. Anyone who knew anything about local football had heard of Stan. He ran the Tigers like his own family.

He blew his whistle and stopped the match. The players came in to him. We could hear him across the pitch, telling each one what he should have done, how he should be passing, where he should be. Laying down the law.

'I wouldn't play under him if you *paid* me,' said Anne.

'*You* haven't been grounded,' I muttered.

I was scared I admit it, but it didn't help Anne telling me what I could see anyway. Everyone said Stan was tough. I also knew they weren't playing well this season and could do with some new players.

Stan blew the whistle and play restarted. We continued watching for a minute or two, while I waited for courage. I was glued to the spot, and that man running up and down the line hollering didn't help. It was the thought of weeks without any football, watching the Perils as a spectator, that forced me forward.

I set off round the pitch. Anne was watching near the gate. She didn't think I would. Well, I would; I would show them all. Hatchback couldn't stop me playing football. While Mum made dolls' houses and Dad watered his marrows, I would score goals. Let them try to stop me.

I got round to Stan's side of the pitch. I caught up with him, and followed behind like a shadow. He didn't see me. All his attention was on the action on the pitch.

Stan wore a dark-red tracksuit, loose-fitting, rather baggy round the knees. Around his neck was a stopwatch and a whistle. His face was red, and his hair thin and grey. He was probably older than Dad.

He wasn't going to notice me in a million years. I would have to call him.

I tried, just as he began a stream of instructions.

'I want to see some passing. Pass, pass, pass – do you know what that means, Alec? That's it. You're part of a team . . . *Be* a team. Don't try to beat 'em all on your own.'

'Sir, excuse me . . . er, sir . . .' I muttered.

The game was taking his total attention.

'You're not six individuals . . . Watch each other. Know

where your mates are . . . Come on, defence, don't fall back . . . Up there, be ready to run in with the attack to catch 'em offside. Effort. Watch, move. See the opening before it happens . . . Pass, pass, pass!' He threw his hands up. 'I might as well be talking to myself.'

I tried again. 'Er, excuse me, sir . . .'

He nearly knocked my head off as he swung an arm round. 'Mark him, Andy. That's more like it. Down the wing, follow through . . . Don't just leave it. What's the point of that? Pass. Then run in ready to take it back.'

One of the boys on the pitch was running towards us.

'Get back in there, John.' He waved him away. 'No time for chit-chat.'

The boy stopped and grinned. 'Keep your hair on, Stan. There's a girl wants to talk to you.'

Stan turned and saw me for the first time. 'Ta, John. Hello, my dear.' He blew his whistle. 'Take five. Then we'll go through the new free-kick combination.'

Play stopped and the boys collapsed on the ground. Stan gave his attention to me, spotlighting me with a smile like a favourite uncle. 'So, what can I do for you, love?'

My tongue was glued in my mouth. Words came out, but I couldn't put much sense in them. 'Well . . . you see . . . I thought . . . I wondered if . . .'

Stan laid an arm on my shoulder. 'Slow down, love. You haven't got a train to catch.'

I took a deep breath, and it came in a rush. 'I'd like to join your team.'

He took his arm off my shoulder, and took half a step back. 'I beg your pardon.'

I had said it once, I could say it again. 'I'd like to join the club, play for you.'

'Play?' he said. 'For Tigers Football Club?'

23

'I'm good,' I insisted. 'Give me a trial.'

Stan grinned, and held up both hands. 'Enough, love. Football is not a game for girls. I know there are a few girls' teams, but to my mind that's all wrong. Unnatural. Football is a hard physical sport. Body contact, fitness, muscle . . . It's a manly sport. Helps boys develop . . . but girls? It's all wrong.'

'There's a Women's Football Association,' I pointed out.

'So what?' He had his hands on his hips. 'There's lions in Trafalgar Square. Look love, why don't you do dancing or gymnastics?'

'Because I want to play football.'

'Not with me you won't.'

'Give me one good reason.'

'One? I'll give you a dozen. Girls aren't fit enough, tough enough . . . They haven't got the bottle. Bit of rain: in they run. Crying, hysterics. Unreliable. You don't want to become aggressive, muscular? You don't want calves like King Kong? No. Let's keep it simple. Men do masculine things, women do feminine things. It's better that way. We all know where we are.'

'You're so wrong . . .' I spluttered

'Not on your life, love. Football is a man's game. Turns boys into men. First bit of mud, in you come. Forget it, love.'

'I'm not your love, and I'm not afraid of mud. I can run as hard as any of that lot. And I can score goals, too.'

Stan was shaking his head laughing. 'This is all too much. Hey lads, come and see what we got here!'

His team began to come over. I could see they were all going to have a go at me.

'So that's it, is it?' I said. 'Can't handle me on your own. Need twelve more, eh?'

'She wants to join the team, lads.'

They were all round me now in their striped shirts.

'She could give out the oranges,' said someone.

'Hang up the net.'

They all joined in now.

'And darn the holes.'

'Wash the kit.'

'And scrape the mud off our boots.'

I looked round at their smarmy faces. 'I hear the Tigers have been losing all their matches.'

That wasn't too bright, at thirteen to one. One of them came in to have a go at me but Stan held him off.

'Take it easy, Cliff. No hitting girls. Let's get back on the pitch. We've wasted enough time. Now darling, I'm sure you've got the message. So run along and get your mum to buy you a new hat.'

I walked a few metres away and then turned.

'Why don't you get yours to buy you a big red nose?'

6

I hardly spoke to Anne on the way home. I know it wasn't her fault, but I just felt so upset. The way all the boys and Stan had had a go at me. I could still see all their faces, telling me I could darn the football net, give the oranges out at half-time, clean their boots . . .

I thought I could join a boys' team and that would be the answer to all my problems. And they wouldn't let me. No, let's be clear on this. Stan wouldn't let me. Stan thinks girls should stand around looking pretty. And all those Tigers are just under his thumb.

Anne tried to be nice, telling me it wouldn't be that long if I just did a bit of schoolwork. She'd get a petition out for me, and so on. I couldn't ask for a better friend, but none of it helped a bit. I was so depressed.

At home I just mooched about. I heard Mum say to Dad, *Just leave her, she's got to get used to it.* Later on Dad asked me if I wanted to go to the zoo at the weekend. I said all right, thinking I might as well keep him happy, but I wasn't in the mood for any zoo. Mum suggested that we had a day at the seaside before it got too cold. I said all right to that, too. And when she suggested a new dress . . . well, really, I just thought of Stan and the last thing he had said to me.

I know they were trying to cheer me up. But it was a bit late. Hadn't they all done their best to make me unhappy? I don't want to watch silly animals in cages, or play with a bucket and spade on a beach. It was like they had taken away a box of chocolates and were offering me a penny lollipop instead.

Try that on a three-year-old, I thought.

That evening I couldn't settle to anything. I tried watching TV but it was the same old stuff. Soaps and quiz shows; all those audiences who laugh at anything. Why do they do that? Are they just silly? Or are their home lives so miserable that going out cheers them up so much they can't stop laughing?

'I can't see anything to laugh at,' I said.

'*You* wouldn't,' said Mum.

'Life is serious,' I said. 'It's about pain and suffering. It's not a joke factory.'

Dad looked at Mum.

'It's not a game,' I said. 'We are not wind-up toys.'

'And that's why,' said Mum, 'you need to improve your schoolwork.'

I didn't say any more. Whatever I said would have been wrong, or they'd have found a connection with schoolwork. So I just lay flat out on the sofa playing with the TV remote. All I seemed to find were programmes with silly people laughing at silly things. I began to flick through at top speed, making my own programme, cutting people off before the punch-line. After a minute or so I sort of knew where I was going. I mixed a bit of that with a bit of this, her with him, these with those . . . Then Mum grabbed the remote off me.

'You're driving me crackers.'

She put the TV on one channel, and took charge of the remote. I watched the programme for two minutes. It was so complicated, what these people had to do, that it was silly. They were answering questions and trying to find each other dressed up in brown paper bags. I don't know why. I didn't *care* why.

27

I went up to my room, and lay on the bed. Mum came up after a while. Then Dad came up. I felt like I was sick in hospital. They should've brought flowers.

They started off being really nice, or trying to be. Offering me fruit and crisps, that sort of stuff. I didn't want none of it. Then promising me more treats, days out here and there and everywhere.

'Keep 'em,' I said.

It was then Mum lost her temper. An ungrateful brat, she called me. Dad said don't shout at her. Mum said *Football, football, football; all she thinks about is football – and you stick up for her.* Then Mum and Dad had a row. And then I felt a bit better, watching them two slug it out. Dad said Mum was neglecting me for dolls' houses, and Mum said he thought more of his monster marrow than he did of me. I wanted to join in, but I thought it safer to watch.

Then I wished I could switch them off. Remote them away. But real-life arguments don't just fit in programme-size slots.

'Can't you fight somewhere else?' I said.

Mum threw a cushion at me, and stormed out. Dad glared at her, then turned to me.

'Now look what you've done!'

I turned into my pillow. 'Good.'

'You little cow,' he exclaimed, banging the door as he left.

So she hated me, he hated me, and I hated them. Fine. I knew where I was now.

Except I didn't, and I started to cry. A little while later Mum came in with milk and biscuits and we had a cuddle. I put my pyjamas on and went down to watch TV, but it really wasn't any better. I just wanted the company.

Later in bed I couldn't sleep. I rolled over and over, thinking of Stan and the Tigers. How I'd like to shoot them!

Thinking of crabby old Natches. Thinking of my ban. How would the Perils play without me? Why should they play without me? I was so miserable that I beat up my pillow, and threw my old teddy into the corner.

I wanted to run away to sea and be a sailor. I wanted to run away to war and be shot. I wanted to . . .

It was already light when the idea hit me. A crazy idea, a stupid idea. An impossible idea. Or was it?

I began to plan it in detail. Maybe, maybe just . . . You never know. It might just work.

7

In the morning I emptied my piggy bank. I had £10.85. That would do.

I set off for school as usual. Mum said she was glad that I had cheered up, and she gave me 50p as I left the house.

I went in the direction of school, but quickly cut off down a side-road. Then a few more roads. I wanted to make sure I didn't meet anyone.

Then I rested for ten minutes on a wall. *Let everyone get safely into school*, I thought. I sat there like I was waiting for someone, looking at my watch every minute or so.

When ten minutes were up, I set off again, and stopped by the nearest phone box. Making sure there was no one I knew about, I went in. I practised the words several times, until I was word perfect. Then, taking a deep breath, I dialled the number.

After the dialling tone came the voice. 'Hello. Hampton Junior School.'

Good, it was the school secretary and not the Head. I couldn't have done it if it was the Head. The secretary I could handle.

'Hello,' I said. 'This is Frances Fairweather's mother. She won't be in today. She has a gippy tummy.'

I crossed my fingers, held my breath, waiting for the reply.

'Thank you for phoning, Mrs Fairweather. I'll tell her class teacher.'

'Thank you,' I said, and put down the phone.

For a few seconds I just stood, amazed at how simple it was. Then I jumped in the air. I had done it. I had put on my mum's voice, and now I had the day to myself to do what I had to.

'Whoopee!' I leapt again, like a goalkeeper punching away a ball. It was when I had landed that I saw a woman outside eyeing me strangely. I calmed down, and left the booth.

'My mum's just had a baby,' I said.

'Congratulations,' she said. 'Boy or girl?'

'Twins,' I said.

I took a bus to the shopping centre. I had some idea what I needed, but also I had time to be fussy. I started with the Oxfam shop. I wanted a jacket, something on the big side.

They had a dark-brown zip-up leather jacket. It was superb. Patched at the elbows, the odd hole here and there, wide across the shoulders; at least a size too big. Just right in fact. And a big canvas bag. Wonderful! I got them both for three pounds.

Now I needed a hat, and it had to be right. I went in four shops, and ended up going back to the first one, a charity shop. It wasn't quite right, but it was the best there was. It fitted close, and had a peak coming down low over my eyes. I tried it in the mirror, but was still unsure. I saw a yellow scarf and put that on with it. Now that was better. Much more like it.

I was about to leave the shop when I saw the wig. My hair is light brown and curly. This was dark brown and straight, with a greasy look. A bit long, but I could trim it. There was hardly anyone in the shop, and the two women at the counter were having a long conversation about the expense of weddings. So I put the wig on, tucking some of the hair under to make it short.

I was about to look in the mirror, when I thought, *No, do*

it properly. I put on the brown jacket. Then I put on the cap, angling it to one side, and only then did I look in the mirror.

I held my arms out a little way from my body. I pressed my feet into the ground, and bent my knees. I'm thin, but the boy looking back at me was stocky and tough in the bulk of the jacket. I swaggered my arms, and he swaggered his. He was tough, swaggering tough, in everything but his face. That was girl-like, and scared.

It was going to be harder than I thought.

8

I came home at the time I normally would after school. Mum was on the phone and Dad was out with his cab. So I went up to my room and hid my gear.

My room's not big. You can't see much of the walls through the football pictures. I've got a West Ham corner with scarves and rosettes and programmes – but I'm thinking of taking that down, and making it a Millwall Lionesses corner. My window faces out on to the garden, and that's half-covered with stickers; you know, supporters club stuff. My bed is under that. Then I've got a chest of drawers and a large built-in cupboard with a mirror in one door. And, apart from a table and chair and a few shelves, that's it.

Frances Fairweather's home ground.

If that makes it sound rather tidy, then imagine the floor pretty well covered up with clothes, boxes, mags – like yours, I suppose. Every time she comes in, Mum goes on at me about it.

Gear stowed, I went down to show my face to Mum. She'd got off the phone and was busy putting lights in a dolls' house, cursing away as the wrong ones went on when she turned on the switches. So I left her to it, and went back upstairs.

I put some drawings out with pens and things just in case she came in. And laid out a few old football mags on the table. With my alibi fixed I had a good look at the wig. The hair was dark brown; it was a woman's wig, straight and quite long. I needed to trim it back so it was more boy-like, but I was frightened to start, knowing what I cut off I couldn't put back. But then again, I couldn't leave it the way it was.

So I took a deep breath and cut off a bit. Just a bit for testers, then I put the wig on. That didn't make much difference. So I cut a bit more off, tried it on – and so on, I was taking it slow. There was no point just hacking at it. It had to be right if I was going to be convincing.

After about an hour I had done what I could. My own hair isn't long, and by trimming it a little I could get it all under the wig.

That was as much as I could do in that direction. I cleaned all the hair cuttings away and put them in a paper bag in a drawer. Now my face. I looked at it in the mirror in the wig. I pushed it about, twisted it this way and that. I had to fit it with my body, or I would just look like Frances Fairweather in fancy dress.

Was it asking too much? I wanted to be taken for a boy from the tip of my toes to the last hair on my head. But I was a girl. And that got me thinking further.

What is a boy? How is he different from a girl? There's hair and dress, but that's only on the surface. And in-between the legs, of course, but that doesn't show. I know men and women aren't the same, but I'm not talking about women and men. How are boys and girls different? I mean really different.

And the more I thought of it, the less I knew. It's no good just saying boys do boys' things and girls do girls' things. That's what Stan had said to me about football. Who decides what boys' things and girls' things are?

Grown-ups.

They decide what is ladylike and what isn't. They decide who can climb trees and who can't. They tell boys and girls

34

what to wear. But they don't seem so clear on that any more. Because girls can wear boys' clothes. I wondered why boys couldn't wear girls' clothes.

I got confused. Do girls walk different, talk different? I just didn't know. And if I didn't know – then there couldn't be that much in it. But I did know if I was going to act as a boy I would have to be different from me, or everyone would know it *was* me.

So, to be convincing, I had to be a different sort of boy than I was a girl. I couldn't just be me dressed up. I had to move, talk and act in another way.

Thinking about it was scary enough. I wondered if I would have the guts to go through with it. That would depend on just how much I wanted to play football.

I went down to have a snack a bit later. I forced myself to watch a bit of TV, so Mum wouldn't wonder what I was up to in my room. Then I went back up. I really wanted to dress up in all the clobber and work on myself with everything on, but I was afraid Mum might walk in. So I just wore the wig. If I heard her coming up I could rip it off quick.

If I push my bed back I can see the whole of myself in the mirror of my built-in cupboard. I stood in front of it. We had these actors come to the school once. And they told us how they worked on a character in a play. I remembered a woman telling us how she acted an old lady. She said she started with the feet and worked up. That didn't make a lot of sense at the time. I remember thinking, *Why the feet: you hardly notice them?*

But I knew now. Your feet are what you stand on. They say what your legs can do. And right up the body, like the song says, 'the foot bone's connected to the ankle bone, the ankle bone's connected to the leg bone . . .' So it has to be feet first. Stands to reason, really.

My feet are boy's feet, I told myself. *My legs are boy's legs* . . .
I worked the feeling up through my body. I imagined it
coming up like a wave and changing me. I became a swag-
gerer, a punch-you-on-the-nose soon-as-look-at-you boy.
Boy from the tip of my toes right up to my chin.

But there was still the face. That's what people look at
when they talk to you – your eyes and your mouth. I looked
at last year's class photo. I couldn't make out any difference
between boys' and girls' faces. The pictures were small, so I
tried again with a magnifying glass. I covered up the hair
with my fingers. You really couldn't tell at all.

It would all come down to how I acted.

I made faces in the mirror. I tried different voices. Deep
ones, high ones. I wanted to put on an accent but found I
couldn't keep it up. Chewing gum helped. It sort of loosened
me up, made me feel more swaggery.

I wisecracked in the mirror, I insulted myself. It was
coming but I had a way to go. I knew it was important to
keep my eyes steady. When you lie, you shift them. I couldn't
do that. I had to hold them straight.

I was called down to dinner. I didn't talk much. Dad had
come home. He and Mum kept trying to draw me out. Like,
How was school today? As you might imagine I did not tell
them I had bunked off. I said it was fine, there were no
problems, and I had worked hard. You know – the usual stuff
to keep parents quiet.

I watched some TV, but soon as I could I went upstairs to
my room. Back to voice practice. I was doing it for a while
when Mum popped in.

'Who are you talking to?' she said.

'I'm practising for a school play,' I said.

'You didn't tell me about that.'

'It's just something us girls are working on,' I said.

36

'Well I want you in bed by 9.30. And how about giving this room a tidy?'

I went to bed at 9.30 but didn't tidy the room. I hadn't time. I went on with my practice in bed. Later on, when I heard Mum and Dad's light go out, I got up. I dressed up in all the gear. Then in front of the mirror I started with my feet.

And as a boy I walked around. I kicked, I scowled, I swaggered, and I thought the words I would be saying. I wanted to talk and shout but was afraid Mum and Dad would hear.

Then I had an idea. I went into my built-in cupboard with a torch. There wasn't a lot of room with all the clothes, and with the boxes of my old toys. Mum had wanted to take them to the guides' jumble sale, but I wouldn't let her. Now I wished she had so I would have had the space.

Too bad.

I sat on a box of stuffed animals, a torch in one hand, a mirror in the other. In went the chewing gum and I talked to myself. I tried to use only words that the boy would use. I had to think of where the boy lived and about his family. I had to think why he would suddenly turn up. I moved about as much as I could with dresses and coats hanging all over me.

I don't know what time I finally got to bed but it was dead late. In the morning Mum had to drag me out of bed. She pushed me about the house, and almost spooned cereal down me.

'Aren't you sleeping?' she said.

'I got a lot to think about,' I said sleepily.

She looked at me in a worried way. 'Maybe I should keep you home.'

I perked up. 'I'm all right.' One day off school was enough to explain away.

I woke up on the way to school. I tried out my swagger on the pavement, and had a go with my face. It was beginning to fit. I had already worked out where I would put all my gear and make my change-over; Dad's shed over the allotment.

After school I would take the stuff there, and set my plan into action.

9

After school I went to Dad's plot over the allotments. They take up the area of a few football pitches, broken up into plots about the size of an average garden, with dirt paths between them. Some of the plots are well-kept up, though looking a bit bare this time of year with all the summer vegetables gone, but there's still lots of beans up their poles and ripening tomatoes. Other plots are pretty weedy, where I imagine people thought that an allotment would be a good idea, but didn't realize you don't just sprinkle seeds and come back in three months to collect the vegetables.

I know all this because I helped Dad out over here when the football season was finished. I did some weeding – that's boring – and I planted seeds – that's more fun. Specially when they come up in a few weeks.

I decided on the allotment for two reasons. Firstly I can't change into a boy at home, I'm bound to get caught. I need somewhere quiet, and Dad's shed fits the bill. The second reason is because the allotments back on to the Tigers' playing-field, and that will cut out how much I'm seen in the streets.

Dad's shed is just like any other shed. Like a big box with a door, a window and a roof. It's made of rough brown planks, dead easy to get splinters off. When I got to it I was surprised to find the door open. I had his spare key, but now I didn't need it. I had a look over his plot to make sure he wasn't there, and decided Dad had just been careless. Pretty careless. Some of the stuff in his shed is well . . . junk, like sacking and old seed boxes, but his tools are worth a bit. He's got a whole wallful of spades, forks, hoes, secateurs, all sorts of stuff. He buys gardening tools the way some people buy cameras.

Not that his shed is tidy, which is another reason why I chose it. Just the tools are tidy. The rest is sort of scattered about. I suppose he tidies up about once a year, but mostly he just wants to work on the plot, and mostly on his marrow.

I hadn't seen the marrow for a few days, and had other things to do than look at it now, but last time I saw it it was massive, like a striped bomb lying in straw. Dad measured it for me; it was 147 centimetres round the middle. Dad is desperate to get those last three centimetres. . . The care he gives the marrow you would not believe.

But I hadn't gone there to think about marrows.

I had my bag of stuff with me. So, taking a deep breath, I started on the transformation. Jeans are jeans so I kept those on. I took my new trainers off, and put on an old white pair. I took out the shoelaces and changed them to a dark-blue pair which made the shoes look a bit odd, but different from what they were. I put on a check shirt Mum had picked up from a jumble but I'd never worn before. Then the brown jacket, zipping up halfway, sort of scruffy casual, the sort you have to work at. Finally the wig. I had a shaving mirror with me, and I adjusted it this way and that, making sure all my hair was in. I twisted my face about and said some words; his words.

Then, from the feet I started. Boys' feet, boys' legs – working the feeling up through my body, out along the shoulders, swaggery shoulders, along bouncing arms, and into a head taking up the same rhythm. I did some knee-bends, some arm-stretches. Not that there was a lot of room in the shed, and it was while I was doing these

40

physical jerks that I happened to look out the window.

And saw Dad. He was by his marrow, and I realized at once why the shed was open. He had been there all along, head down doing his thing to his monster. I pulled out of view and watched him. He had a bucket of stuff and a bit of hose-piping. What was he up to?

Whatever it was, he certainly wasn't coming in the shed for a while. I tidied up Frances' clothing, shoved them in the bag and under a pile of sacking. Then I took another look at Dad. He was looking about shiftily as he fitted one end of the hose into the bucket and the other end in the marrow.

Then I knocked over a can of nails. Dad shot up in panic and I shot out of the shed.

'Oi! What you doing in there?' he yelled.

I didn't hang around to answer. I just belted for it. Straight across plots, down rows of tomatoes and cabbages. Dad would want to know what I was up to if he caught me, and that would be the end of it. I just had to get away.

The trouble was, Dad was between me and the gate. And coming for me.

I didn't know whether I could outrun Dad or not. I never used to be able to, but over the last year I've put on a lot of speed, so this would be my chance to find out.

I lost him behind a row of beans. I stayed where I was, hoping to pull him away so I could get round him, but when I looked again there he was, doing the same thing, waiting me out.

In the end I made a run for it, and he came for me. Before he'd been edging round the plots, but this time he was in for the kill, tearing across the plots like a raging rhino. If he caught me I was going to get it one way or the other, no matter *who* I was.

I was tiring, and he had the advantage there, as I'd been

going twice his distance at the beginning trying to get round him, but without getting anywhere.

I made it to a shed, and ducked round the back. I could hear him running to it, and I thought, *That's it – he's got me now*. He was either going to wait for me to come round or was going to make a rush. I was just too far from the gate and too whacked. All the trouble I had gone to was about to come to nothing. All the money I had spent, all the practice . . . I sat on the ground and wanted to cry.

I heard a distant clang of a gate. Company for Dad.

I had bungled it first time out. I had wanted to be a big brave boy but I was little old Frances Fairweather all along, who couldn't even fool a marrow.

In a little while I was still sitting there, and wondered why Dad hadn't got me. I'd just been sitting waiting. I stood up. Where was he?

I peered round the shed, and to my surprise saw Dad up near the gate talking to another man. It didn't make sense – why hadn't he got me after chasing me so far?

Why – when he had been so close – had he let me go?

Because that man had come. But so what? Because – and then it hit me – he didn't want the man to know what he was doing to his marrow. Dad had been in the middle of doing it when he came after me.

He *was* doing something he shouldn't.

And that made two of us.

I made my way round sheds, through beanpoles, going wide past the two of them, crouching low. If Dad saw me he was no longer interested, and in a few minutes I was out of the allotment gate.

I had a clear choice now. Chuck it in – or do it.

I became Frank going down the field to the Tigers' hut. Walking at just the right pace, watching the practice. Feet right, body right, swinging away. I stopped and watched the players, real casual. Daring one of them to say, *It's that girl*, but no one did. I watched the play for a couple of minutes, and wasn't that impressed. It was a practice match, and not a lot better than playground stuff. I thought they were sloppy. Too much chasing about and not enough marking.

But then Stan wasn't about, and you can't play every session like a match. I'd let them off this once.

I made my way to the hut. Frank's way; cool, like I had all the time in the world, and more than half its confidence. None of which could be further from the truth. My body was running with electricity. It was killing me to act casual.

The door of the shed was open and as I got near I could hear voices. I thought I'd wait for a break in the conversation. You know manners! Stan was talking to his captain, who I gathered was called Cliff. I couldn't see them as they were well in the hut, but as the talking went on I began to get interested.

'So, last Saturday's match . . .' said Stan.

'Not good, was it?' mumbled Cliff.

'Lousy.'

'All right, it was lousy.'

Someone was striding about, and as he came past the door I saw it was Stan. He ignored me, so I came a little way into the hut and leaned against the door-frame watching them.

Cliff, tall and thin, in training gear, was looking out the window at the match on the field. It was obvious where he really wanted to be.

Stan turned to me. 'You want something, son?'

'Yeah,' I said, as cocky as I dared be. 'I want a word.'

'Hang on a minute, boy.'

As he didn't ask me to leave, I stayed where I was, leaning against the frame.

'So what we gonna do?' asked Stan.

Cliff scratched his neck. 'I've been thinking. That four-two-four line-up . . . What if we switched to three in the attack, five midfield and two backs?'

Stan shook his head. 'It's not the system. It's the work-rate. We've got to pull out the lazy players.'

Cliff looked out the window again. It was so plain he didn't want to be in the hut taking the punishment. It's why I'd never be captain. He just wanted to kick a ball. Me and you both, Cliff.

'So who we gonna drop then?' asked Cliff, turning to him.

Stan smiled as Cliff spoke. 'It's not as simple as dropping, lad.' He punched a fist into a palm. 'We need a player in the front line with some buzz . . .'

What a line! How could I miss it?

'You talking about me?' I said, swaggering into the shed.

'What?' said Stan eyeing me over.

I strode around the room. 'Buzz you want? That's me.'

There was no way back. I had to keep it going.

'Who are you?' said Stan at last.

'Frank Storm,' I said. 'The lightning striker! I'm gonna transform your team.'

'How?'

I was looking up at the ceiling, as if my eyes could raise it. 'By scoring.'

'And how will you do that?'

I shone Stan a brilliant smile. 'By being . . . there.'

'Where?'

'Where it's at.'

As I said it, I picked up a football and dropped it on my toe. Knee to toe I went with the ball half a dozen times. The sort of stuff I do all the time with Anne. I can't say it's that useful on the pitch but it looks good. To finish off I gave the ball a little flick in the air, and with my left foot whammed it straight out the door.

Stan pursed his lips. 'Nice control.'

Cliff said, 'Who you played for?'

I jumped to the ceiling and headed an imaginary ball through the window.

'I just moved down from up North,' I said.

'So who was it then?' he said.

I spun round with a forefinger pointing at Cliff's face. 'Don't give me the third degree, sonny . . . Do you want me or not?'

'Yes we do,' said Stan quietly.

Cliff said, 'How do we know what he's like?'

Stan did what he normally did. He ignored his captain. 'Frank,' he said. 'Frank Storm – you be at Wanstead Flats changing room at 9.45 Saturday morning.'

I extended my hand. 'Righto, guv. You won't regret this.' We shook hands. I turned to Cliff, tall lanky Cliff who was pressed against the shed wall. He didn't look at all pleased.

'Who's your monkey?' I said to Stan.

'The team captain,' said Stan.

I looked him up and down. 'Pleased to meet you, I'm sure.'

'Yeah . . .' said Cliff, who hadn't moved.

'Didn't you used to play for the Jelly Babies?'

45

'Not me,' said Cliff.

I screwed up my eyes like I was wondering whether I knew him. 'Must've been your brother then.' I turned to Stan. 'Been nice meeting ya fellas. I'm gonna transform the Tigers. You'll wonder how you ever did without me.' I swung away. 'See ya, then. Don't do nothing I wouldn't, eh?'

And then I left them. Making my way, oh so cool, down that pitch. I could feel the pair of them watching. Well, I had all the time in the world now.

I was a Tigers' player.

11

I left the park and couldn't believe it. They'd taken me on. But there was no way I could have stayed for the training session. I was boiling like a pot of soup. I needed a fortnight's holiday.

But who'd believe it? Saturday I was playing for them. The Tigers! The excitement was killing. My nerves were buzzing like pylon wires.

The worst bit was Dad over the allotment. I really thought I'd had it then. I mean, some people I can fool, but give me a few weeks (please!) before I have to face Dad.

I couldn't get over my cheek with the Tigers. Once I started, I just let it run. Not that I could have stopped. I was so high on nerves that the words seemed to be just waiting to be said. I didn't have to think.

A Tigers player!

All that work the previous night paid off. All that talking to myself, that walking around the room . . . I decided that I must work on it again that evening. I needed the words inside me so that I could deal with any situation . . . Like the match on Saturday. That wouldn't be just walking in and out of a room. I'd have to face the whole team.

Boy!

But football at the weekend, that's what made my heart sing. A match! I'd show those Tigers a thing or two. You'd see if I wouldn't.

But it wasn't the weekend for a few days. And I was drained, like I'd just played a double Cup Final with extra time. Just those five minutes with Stan and Cliff had emptied my tanks.

I went back to the allotment – and made double certain Dad wasn't there before going over to the shed. He'd locked up this time. I opened up, got out Frances' stuff from under the pile of sacking, and became me again.

What a relief!

12

The next couple of days I spent preparing myself for the game with the Tigers. I would have to play good football and at the same time be accepted as a boy. I wasn't that worried about the football, as I had seen their training and I thought I was as good as most. But being Frank *and* playing good football . . . Together, that would be a real test.

I thought about nothing else.

When I could I practised being Frank. It wasn't till late at night that I could put on the full gear, but earlier in the evening I worked with the wig, ready to whip it off if I heard a sound on the stairs.

I experimented with make-up. If I got rid of my freckles on my nose and cheeks, and darkened my eyebrows, I found I looked less like Frances. I knew that Stan and Cliff had seen me with freckles, but they'd only seen me once and not for very long. And if I didn't overdo it, they wouldn't notice. I knew it was doing things in the wrong order, but then I couldn't always think of them in the right order.

Then I came to the big problem.

The wig.

I went out on the Flats with my wig in my bag. I got as far away from anybody else as I could and practised headers with it on. Each time I would look in the shaving mirror and see if it moved.

And it did, and sometimes I knocked it clean off. I tried heading in different ways, and some ways shifted the wig less than others – but it was impossible to say for sure what would happen. I score half my goals with my head. Just imagine if I scored and my wig came off!

That would get a cheer all right.

No – my wig would have to stay on through thick and thin or I'd be ducking away from the high balls.

Back home I tried glue. Useless. Sellotape, Blue-Tack, paper-clips, hair slides; by themselves, together, in all sorts of combinations. Useless. I began to get desperate and thought of filling the wig up with cement.

I spent half my pocket money on a roll of sticking-plaster, and it didn't work at all. It was only sticky on one side. Mum uses double-sided tape in her dolls' houses, for sticking on wallpaper and things like that. I got some of hers, but it was too thin and not sticky enough. I needed something like double-sided sticking-plaster. Wide and strong and very sticky.

I went back to my roll of sticking-plaster. It was three centimetres wide, and I tried to sew it back to back. This had me in tears. You try sewing something that is sticky on both sides. It stuck to my fingers, it stuck to the thread, it stuck to the bedclothes – it stuck to itself.

I chucked the whole mess of it in the bin.

On Friday morning eating breakfast with Dad I was still worrying about that wig. I'd hardly slept, thinking about cotton, string, rope, superglue (that's if I never wanted to get the wig off again).

It was when I was sticking two bits of toast together with egg yolk that Dad asked, 'Got a problem?'

I said, 'I need something sticky for school. A model I'm making. I have to put a wig on it. And the model is going to be moved a lot.'

'What sort of model?'

'An astronaut,' Not bad for spur-of-the-moment. 'How can I stop the wig shifting?'

Dad thought for a moment. 'Elastic?'

'No good. It slips.'

'What you doing with this astronaut?'

'It's the helmet,' I said. 'When we take it off, it takes the wig off.'

'Ah,' said Dad, and I breathed easily. Frank was teaching me to be a good liar. He snapped his fingers. '*I* know what you want.'

Dad went off to his tool cupboard and came back with a roll of tape.

'Carpet tape,' he said, and then demonstrated. It was like the stuff I had been trying to sew together. Maybe someone else had the same problem. It was double-sided fabric tape that you stick under a carpet edge to hold it down. The top sticks to the carpet and the bottom to the floor.

I gave Dad a hug and went out whooping to school.

Lunchtime I came home. I don't normally, as I take a packed lunch, but I had to try out that tape. Mum and Dad were both out luckily, so no hassles there. I went up to my bedroom, cut off a length of the tape and stuck it inside the wig. Then put it on my head.

And it worked. The wig clung like a limpet to my skull.

Mind you, getting it off wasn't fun. It hurt like ripping a plaster off, and left rubbery bits round my head. But that was trivial.

Now Frank could head balls into the net.

13

The match on Saturday had another big problem. A problem no amount of sticky tape would solve. And that was changing. If I had had the Tigers colours I could've come along in them, but I didn't have them. Stan would give them to me before the match, and then I would have to go in the boys' changing room and get changed.

I didn't fancy that at all.

At school we get changed with the boys. That is, in the classroom before PE and games. But at school there are a load of girls as well as the boys. Over Wanstead Flats there would be just me. And I'd never been in a boys' changing room before. What did they do in it? On their own.

It didn't bear thinking about.

I went out the day before and bought a pair of boys' pants. The woman looked at me a bit funny, and I said they were for my brother. I knew she was wondering why a sister would be buying her brother a pair of pants, and it was on the tip of my tongue to say my mum was dead . . . But that was a lie I couldn't tell. So I left her to think what she liked.

Money was getting short now, and I was relieved that I didn't have to buy a vest as well. I could have just afforded one, but when I looked them over in the shop I saw they were no different to some plain ones I had already.

Saturday morning of the match, in my bedroom, I put on a vest and the pants I had bought. Over them I wore football shorts and a shirt, not Tigers colours, but just temporary for the journey. And over them a tracksuit. On my feet I wore a

52

pair of trainers and no socks. My plan was to cut changing to the minimum.

I left home saying I was going for a kick-about on the Flats.

Now that was almost true. I was most certainly going over the Flats. And I would do some kicking. I suppose it was the bits that I missed out that were the lie.

I went over the allotment first.

In Dad's shed I made the changes. I was a bundle of nerves. Today I wouldn't have the protection of Frank's clothes. Not that it would help much if I did. I would have to take them off for the game, so it hardly mattered if I didn't go in them. Besides, the less time I had to spend in the boys' changing room the better.

I made room on a shelf for the shaving mirror and started with the make-up. My hands were trembling. I stopped and counted to twenty. It didn't help; I would have to put my make-up on with the shakes. It was just simple colouring to cover my freckles, and darkener on my eyebrows. Nothing fancy; it was important it didn't show.

My eyebrows came out a bit messy but I tidied them up with a flannel. Then I put on the wig, taping it on the inside first. I tested it for strength – firm!

Then I put everything away and set off for Wanstead Flats.

53

14

Stan had said 9.45 outside the changing room. That was for a ten o'clock kick-off. My idea was to get there at five to ten. That might annoy Stan, but the changing room would be emptier and by the time I was changed the game would be ready to start.

I jogged to Wanstead Flats from the allotment as I would barely have time for a warm-up. Stan glared at me as I came into the car park.

'What time d'you call this?'

'Same time you call it.' Frank was off to his usual cheek.

'9.45 means 9.45 in my book,' said Stan angrily.

'I must read it sometime.'

He stood open-mouthed as if about to deliver some enormous lecture, but time was on my side.

'Get in,' he ordered.

Stan led me into the changing room. We went along the corridor to where the team had a small side-room with benches round the walls and pegs above. There were only three boys in the room, the others already on the pitch.

Stan handed me a set of Tigers gear.

'Get changed quick, and out.' He left me.

I put my bag up on the hook, shaking with nerves. I wished I could stop. I began to undo my shoes.

'Who are you?' said a dark-haired boy.

I looked up. 'Who are you?'

'I asked first,' he said.

The three boys were looking at me.

'Don't your captain tell you anything?' I said, taking off my shoes. 'I'm referee.'

That got a laugh. And when it was over, I said, 'I'm Frank to my friends, but you can call me sir.'

I was sounding like a Christmas cracker.

Stan came in at that instant and ordered us to hurry up.

I said, 'Make 'em wait.'

Stan growled. 'A ten o'clock kick-off means a ten o'clock kick-off.'

'That in your book?' I asked perkily. 'What chapter?'

'Cut the wisecracks. You got three minutes.' He left the room, slamming the door.

I took the hint. I pulled off my tracksuit top and put on the Tigers shirt. It was on the big side, but that had the advantage of hanging low on my body as I took off my tracksuit bottoms and shorts.

I felt the three boys were watching me, but when I looked up, they weren't, of course. With only a couple of minutes to kick-off, they had plenty to concentrate on.

Once I had the shorts on I felt easier. I put the socks on, slipped in my shin pads and then got my boots out of my bag. By this time I was alone. I wanted to be Frank, but felt very much like Frances, and hoped the football would take me over.

I did the laces up and said a quick prayer. 'Please God, make me Frank.'

Leaving the changing room I realized I needed a pee. I had gone before I left home but my nerves had worked on me since. I hesitated in the corridor, and wondered whether I could hold it. I started for the entrance then stopped. I had come here to play football, and knew there was no way I could play a decent game without going to the toilet.

'Where's the loo?' I said to a man heading for the outside.

He pointed. And I went.

Inside there were a couple of boys with their backs to me standing before the urinals. I looked about helplessly, then saw the cubicles. I belted into one and locked myself in. I wiped the seat with some toilet paper and had my pee. Sitting on the seat I checked my wig and wondered what I was doing. A gents' loo, for heaven's sake!

I closed my eyes and tried to calm down. I felt about three years old. Around me, doors were banging and water gurgling. Every sound was terrifying – as if outside that door was every possible enemy, waiting for me to come out.

I stood up and tidied my clothes. Frank's feet I began, Frank's legs, Frank's body, arms, legs. I am Frank, Frank, Frank, I burned into my head. Frank the lad, Frank the bullet, Frank the demon striker. And in that instant of courage I belted out of the cubicle, and out of the loo.

Stan was waiting for me outside.

'Pitch number eleven,' he said impatiently. 'Let's go.'

The morning was sunny, still a little chilly, but warming up. *Not a bad morning for football*, I thought as we weaved between the pitches to get to ours. The mist had lifted, and all around were football matches in progress as far as the eye could see.

Stan was about to say something, so I decided to get in first.

'Who was the only member of the Royal family sent off in a Cup Final?'

Stan shook his head without looking at me.

'Don't you want to know?' I said.

'Save the jokes,' he said.

'That's what I like about you, Stan,' I said. 'Your rich sense of humour.'

By then, we were at the pitch. Both teams were kicking

about round their goals. I jogged over to join the Tigers. I had a couple of kicks of the ball, touched my toes and did a bit of arm-swinging.

Cliff came over. 'You all right for centre forward, Frank?'

'Yeah.'

That was as much as I got from him because then the referee blew his whistle and the two teams got into position. The referee tossed up, Cliff called and lost. It was their kick-off.

The ref blew up and play started. I felt I had been playing ninety minutes already.

It was a scrappy game, and I can't say the opposition were much good. But then the Tigers weren't so hot either. I spent the first twenty minutes getting to know how they worked. There's no point rushing into position if nothing is going to come to you.

There was Cliff and John on either side of me, and also Duke and Mohun on the wings. As I got to know them a bit I had a quick word. I needed some fast balls up centre where I could use my speed and ball skills.

Towards the end of the first half we began to take over the game. In the twenty-third minute, Duke had the ball on the right wing and brought it well into their half. I raced through into some space. Duke crossed it to Cliff. I yelled for it and Cliff sent it forward. I had a run-in with one of their defenders and got there first. I beat him on a dummy and socked it from four metres out.

Goal!

First one for the Tigers. I did my goal run, and the lads came up, slapping me on the back. I could see Stan on the sideline beaming. I gave him my raised fist and he gave me one back.

One up.

I had another chance five minutes later. This was from a corner kick taken by Ahmed. He slapped it high and I came in before goal and got a head to it. It went outside the post by centimetres.

But what pleased me more was my wig staying on.

At half-time Stan was all smiles. 'Brilliant goal, lad. And dead close with that header.'

He handed round the half-oranges, and while we were slurping he gave us the pep talk. Telling us to keep pushing forward, and to get lots up front for me. He slapped me on the back a couple of times and I thought, *Just don't pull my hair*.

I wasn't comfortable amongst all the team. They all seemed to be giving me the once-over. Or even twice-over. Was my make-up patchy, I wondered? I daren't adjust the wig.

'What hair cream do you use?' said John.

'Motorbike oil,' I said.

'I bet you do,' said Stan looking at my hair. 'So tell me . . .'

'What?' I said warily, hoping he hadn't spotted the wig.

'Who *was* the only member of the royal family sent off during a Cup Final?'

'Joe Royal,' I said with relief. Stan looked puzzled. 'Think about it,' I said as I jogged back on pitch.

In the second half, it was Tigers all the way. John scored after ten minutes, and after twenty I got a cross from Mohun centre field. I made ten metres and sent it to Cliff, and the pair of us zipped through them, sending the ball back and forth. Cliff had the shot, and it came back off the post. And bingo – I was up in the air, heading it straight in the net.

Not only a goal – but I'd kept my hair on!

3–0.

Then we seemed to slacken off a bit, and they pulled a goal back. Cliff got a bit angry at this, and Stan was doing his nut on the sidelines, but I thought, *So let them have one*.

With two minutes to go I was inside the penalty area, and three defenders were coming at me. It had to be a quick left-foot shot. Wham! It was that close it must've taken the paint off the post.

When the final whistle went it was 3–1. Good enough.

I didn't stick around for any victory ceremony but ran straight back to the changing room. I took off my boots, put on my tracksuit, slipped on my trainers, and had all my gear in my bag by the time the lads got in.

'Sorry, Cliff,' I said.

'Why's that?'

'It's a long time since I only scored two.'

That got a laugh, which was my leaving present. I couldn't stay in the room with that lot dropping their shorts! I shot out with my bag and bumped into John in the corridor.

'Ain't you staying?' he exclaimed. 'Stan's taking us up McDonald's.'

'Got another match in ten minutes,' I said and slipped out.

And hoped that was it. But no – Stan was outside and he was all over me. 'Marvellous, Frank. You took 'em apart . . . Beautiful to watch.'

'Like a load of schoolgirls,' I said.

'Eh, Frank – talking of girls, we had one tried to join us, middle of the week. You'd've laughed, mate . . .'

And the worst of Frank burst out of me. Like he'd had enough of the practice, and it just had to come.

'It's a man's game,' I said, flexing my muscles. 'Turns boys into men.'

'Exactly what I said.'

'Girls with muscles.' I punched the air. 'Who wants them?'

'We think alike, lad,' Stan said. 'Here's some horse liniment. Rub it in those legs . . . They're gold. Now go and get a shower with the rest of the team . . .'

'Er . . . don't think I will, Stan. Prefer a bath.'

'Well stick around. I'm treating the team.'

But I was already off. 'Can't stay,' I called. 'Me mum's got a cow pie on the table . . . See ya.'

And I went. Straight to the allotment. I stopped once to take the wig off in case anyone might see me. I sat on a wall wincing like the little pig going to market. Whatever that tape did to carpets, it certainly didn't want to let go of me.

In the shed I wiped off the make-up and changed back.

Some morning! I was wiped out. The match was the easy bit. I'd had an early start, and too many late-night sessions, but it was being Frank – living on my nerves, not knowing what was going to happen next – that drained me.

Still, two goals; that was something. I did a victory whoop on the street.

If only they knew . . .

As I came in, Dad called out, 'Good session?'

'Oh just a kick-about.'

I didn't stick around to discuss it, but went straight off to have a bath. I had the hottest and longest soak I'd had in years.

15

I didn't see much of Frances in the next week or two. I wondered if she was avoiding me, but then I thought, *That can't be.* I am her best friend after all. Maybe she just doesn't want to talk football with anyone. I mean, I am the captain of the Perils, and I'd have to tell her who we were replacing her with for the St Mary's match. Alice – and she wasn't much good. Nor were any of us. I think we'd started to rely too much on Frances. We lost 2–0 to St Mary's.

I don't know whether that would have cheered Frances up or not. She still couldn't play for us whether we won or lost. I did see her in class of course, and she seems to be working harder. So maybe Frances has just decided that the only way she is going to play football is to improve her work. I must admit, it did surprise me, seeing her with her head down, working away. Even *maths* she was doing.

We still had our kick-abouts at playtime, and when I asked her what she was doing after school she just said this and that. And I thought, *That means nothing, and she doesn't want to admit it.*

I was hurt, though, when I went round to her house a few times, and her mum told me she was out. I wondered, *Is she really out, and if so – what is she doing? Or is it she just doesn't want to see me?*

I thought, *Give her her own time.* We'll be friends again soon, but she has got to get used to the fact that she can't play football and I can. I do miss her though. We used to have such a lot of fun. She was the only one who really knew what I was talking about. She understood what I dreamt about.

I'm nowhere near as good at football as she is. I'm the reliable type. You can always count on Anne, they say. I always turn up for practice. I work hard during a game, but I never shine. Not that I'm a bad player, I'm just not a very good one. I wish I was. I wish I had Frances' speed, I wish I could get up in the air like she can, and twist and turn in a tackle.

I dream I am really good. I dream I find a ring and it gives me a wish. And I wish to be the best footballer, and suddenly I am so good that no one can believe it. Everyone wants me to play for them, everyone wants to talk to me. And I have to make a decision whether to play for England men's or England women's team. It's on the news, and in the newspapers. 'What will Anne Harper decide?' ask the headlines. In the end I play for both.

The reason I'm captain of the Perils is that I'm bossy. I can get the girls, most of them anyway, to come to training and organize them for matches. Frances can't do that. She'd just be thinking about herself, and forget about the others, whereas I tell everyone three times, and even drag them along to team practice. My opinion is that if you don't practise you shouldn't play in the matches. The trouble is that we can't say that because we've only just got enough players.

Straight after the match I wrote up the petition for Frances. It said:

We think it is unfair that Frances Fairweather can't play for the Perils because of her schoolwork. She is a good footballer and we don't believe that schoolwork and being in the girls' football team should have anything to do with each other. We demand she comes back in the team immediately.

My mum suggested that last sentence. I first wrote 'We want her back in the team . . .', but Mum said, 'No, you're the team, be tougher about what you want.' She suggested the word 'demand'. It sounded a bit tough to say to a teacher. 'Go on,' says Mum. So I did.

My mum works in the hospital, and she's a shop steward in her trade union. She said, 'Don't let them walk over you. But make sure you know what to do if they *don't* give Frances her place back.'

I talked that over with the girls. The obvious thing was not to play in the team: to just say we won't play unless Frances can play. That could cause us problems though. Because we'd have to do it just before a match, or it just wouldn't matter. And if we did, then the match would have to be cancelled, and then who would want to play us?

As far as I could see, that left only one other possibility: the one me and Frances had already thought about. We'd start our own team, a team that would have nothing to do with school. The idea got everyone excited. No teachers organizing sessions and telling us what to do. It would be all us, just our say-so.

But then I got to think about it, and I know that some of the girls – although they won't admit it – need telling what to do. And if we started our own team, who would do that? Who's the only one bossy enough?

I was going to get lumbered with a lot of work.

The team liked the idea, though, and I said I'd look at how we could do it: who we'd play with and all that. I'm going to write to the Women's Football Association and tell them the problem.

Then, while we were all together, I got all the girls to sign the petition, and a little later I gave it to Ms Natches. She read it, and didn't say anything for a while. Then read it again. Finally she said she'd like to talk to me about it after school. I agreed.

I stayed after class. I was nervous, and wished I'd asked one of the other girls to stay with me. It's difficult standing up to a teacher.

Ms Natches closed the classroom door, and then sat down with me.

'I was very sad to read this,' she said.

I didn't answer.

'It hurt me a lot,' she said.

And, looking at her, I could see it did. She wasn't being heavy, just telling me how she felt.

I said, 'If we'd have had Frances we'd have beaten St Mary's.'

She sighed, and said, 'Anne, lovey, I'm a teacher. If I was just your football manager, then things would be different. But I am also your teacher.'

I said, 'It's not fair . . .'

'I could let Frances carry on as she is now. Just let her completely neglect her work, and say – well it's her life. But Frances is ten years old, and there's lots she doesn't know about the world. That's why she goes to school. And she's got at least six more years of it. If I just let her be lazy, let her muck about – then school will be a waste of time. She'll get no qualifications, and end up stacking shelves in a supermarket.'

'She might play professional football,' I said.

'There isn't any for women,' said Ms Natches.

'There is in Italy.'

Ms Natches threw up her hands. 'Far be it for me to

64

discourage her. Girls should do what they want. And maybe she'll go to Italy... Will working at school do her any harm?'

I agreed it wouldn't.

'And it might do her some good?'

I had to say yes.

'I haven't got it in for Frances, you know. But I *am* her teacher.'

I could see her point of view. It was complicated, and yet it still didn't seem fair. I remembered the way we had all felt after the St Mary's game. It seems to me you either choose your best team or you don't play at all.

Ms Natches said, 'What will the team do if I continue not allowing Frances to play?'

'Some of the girls said they won't play any more,' I said.

'That would make it difficult for me. I know you think I'm not doing much, but I am trying hard to get matches for the Perils. Tonight I've got a meeting where I'm trying to set up a special match. I don't want to tell you about it now, because it's not settled yet. But if I don't have a team it's a waste of my time.'

I didn't say anything. I felt confused. Of course I wanted the Perils to do well, and play other teams, but did that have to mean I couldn't stand up for my friend?

Teacher said, 'I don't want to quarrel with you, Anne. You are a good team captain, and I know you want the best for the team. And so do I.' She stopped, and took a breath. 'Look, I'll come halfway. If you can convince Frances that school is the place for schoolwork... then, in view of this special game, I might give her her place back.'

'I'll talk to her,' I said.

16

After tea I decided to go and see Frances. I would tell her what Ms Natches had said. It was a pity she had said 'might let her play'. 'Might' didn't mean she *would* let her. Still, it was better than nothing, and she seemed to be suggesting that if Frances pulled her socks up she 'might' (that word again!) be playing soon.

I wondered what the special match was.

I turned on to Frances' road, and I saw this boy come past her house. He was walking towards me, bouncing on his heels, and swinging his shoulders. He was wearing a brown leather jacket, and had dark greasy hair poking out of a cap pulled over his eyes. As he got closer I stopped. I couldn't make it out as he came swaggering towards me, but there was something about him . . . It was difficult to say just what.

When he got near, he said, 'You wouldn't know the way to Wanstead Flats, would you?'

'Frances!' I exclaimed.

The boy took a step back. 'What?'

'You're Frances,' I said.

'Now look,' said the boy. 'All I did was ask you the way to Wanstead Flats . . .'

'Oh stop it, Frances.'

'Stop it yourself.'

'You are Frances, aren't you?'

He stood back, arms folded, grinning. 'You got this Frances on the brain, ain't you?'

'I know it's you,' I said, a bit less sure.

'What colour hair your mate got?'

'Light brown?'

'Now you wouldn't call this light brown, would you?'

'No . . .'

'As it happens, I know your Frances . . . Got freckles, right?'

I nodded.

'See mine?'

I couldn't, and yet . . . He was so like her. What was it? The eyes. They were definitely her eyes.

'You can't kid me,' I said.

'Look darling, the name's Frank. And if you want proof, ask me mum.'

I kept staring at him. He moved differently, and Frances' hair and colouring were not the same but the details were. The shape of her mouth and nose, and her fingernails; Frances' are rounded and she bites them a bit. There couldn't be two people with the same fingernails.

I would've bet my life he was Frances.

But then I thought, *Two can play this game; we'll see how she likes it.*

'Sorry,' I said, pretending I had accepted him. 'It's just you look so alike. So what was the question you asked?'

'Forget it,' he sniffed.

I shrugged. 'I said I was sorry.'

He, she, oh you-know, pulled his cap further down, and sucked in his cheeks. 'Anyone ever tell you you're beautiful?' he said.

'No,' I said.

'Not surprised.'

'Ooh, you think you're so smart, don't you?'

'Come to think of it . . . yeah, I do. And good-looking. But then I got to hand it to you.'

'Why's that?'

'You'd never catch it otherwise.'

All right, Frances, I thought, *you play clever and I'll play it cleverer.*

He walked round me, looking me up and down. 'My girlfriend says you play football.'

'Who's your girlfriend?'

'Ever hear of the . . .' he stopped for a second and winked, '. . . the Perils Football Club?'

'Might have,' I said, giving nothing away.

'Know their ace striker?' he said pulling his cap down further.

'Frances Fairweather.' And thought, *That's you. No matter what you say and do.*

'You don't half look like her,' I added.

'That's 'cos we're mates.' He looked at me smugly, and crossed his fingers. 'Best mates.'

'How come I never seen you together?' I said, matter-of-fact.

'We're always together,' he said. 'Nowadays.'

'You ain't now,' I said, knowing they couldn't be *more* together!

'Seen her around much?'

'Well . . .' I hesitated, 'not the last couple of weeks . . .'

'That's 'cos she's been with me.'

'So?' I said.

He suddenly stopped his bouncing about. 'I thought you were her best mate.'

'Was,' I said.

'What d'yer mean "was"?'

Now it was my turn and I hit back hard. 'Things change,' I said. 'I got fed up waiting. You can only knock on someone's door so long. If they're never in, you get to thinking it's time

68

to stop coming round . . . and find new friends.'

After a pause he said, 'So who's your best friend now, then?'

'Alice,' I said.

He looked away, and without looking back said quietly, 'She still likes you, you know.'

'Who?'

'Frances.'

'Bully for her.'

'If you like,' he began, still avoiding my eyes, 'I could get the two of you back together.'

I shrugged. 'Who says I want to?'

Half of me wanted to say, *Stop this game, I know who you are*, and the other half thought, *No, she's mucked me about enough; let her suffer now.*

He said, 'You got a few minutes?'

I shrugged. 'Maybe.'

'I want to show you something.' He looked at me, and saw I was still undecided. 'Something important.'

'All right,' I said curiously.

We set off together.

17

He took me over the allotments. We hardly spoke on the way. I suppose he, or she, Frank Frances – I hardly know what to call him – had enough to think about.

He led me between the plots, and finally stopped at a shed. He took out a key and opened up.

'Wait outside a minute, will you?'

I said I would. He went in and closed the door. I tried to listen to what was going on inside but couldn't hear much. I looked through the keyhole but could only see a bit of movement that made no sense.

So I sat on the step and drew patterns in the dust. I wondered whether I had overdone it; saying Alice was my best friend, and how Frances didn't matter to me at all. But then she had hurt me. She had just thought I'd be there waiting when she stopped doing whatever she was doing.

If you want a friend, Frances, I thought, *then* be *a friend.*

But then there were two sides to that. What I was doing now couldn't exactly be described as friendly. I wanted to hurt. I was trying to say, *This is what it feels like to be chucked over for no reason. Don't expect me to be always waiting for you.*

I picked up a handful of dust and let it fall between my fingers. And thought, *She's a long time.* I had an instant of panic, and wondered whether there was another way out. That would be just like Frances to leave me sitting in the middle of nowhere. I jumped up and ran round the shed.

Phew! There was only one door.

And out of it, a minute later, came Frances!

18

When I went with Anne to the allotment I didn't know what I was going to do. She'd upset me with all that stuff about her and Alice. And now I didn't want her to go away, but I didn't want to tell her or anybody else about Frank.

He was my problem.

I left her outside the shed and changed to Frances. I didn't know how I was going to explain away his disappearance. It was stupid of me to bring her.

'Hello,' I said, as I came out.

'Have you left him in there?' asked Anne.

'Yes.'

'Won't he get tired?' she said, giving me a sarcastic look.

I bit my lip and said, 'You know, don't you.'

She nodded.

'Damn!' I exclaimed. 'I thought I was really good at him.'

'You had me half-fooled,' she said.

I looked away and wondered why it had been so important to fool Anne. Why did it hurt that I hadn't? Was it just my pride? Or was it his?

Anne held me by the shoulders and looked me up and down. 'Some friend you are!'

'I'm sorry,' I said.

She crossed her arms. 'I bet you are.'

I hesitated and then said, 'Is it true about Alice?'

'What do *you* think?'

'Don't know. But I deserve it.'

'You most certainly do!' exclaimed Anne. 'Do you think

I'm just a bit of furniture you can pick up and put down?'

'I didn't mean it,' I said shamefully. 'I get in his clothes and say things and do things . . .' I stopped. 'They were all rubbish, Anne. You're my best friend.'

'Was,' she said.

'Oh don't say that!' I felt tears welling.

'I hate you sometimes,' she said.

And I looked at her, and she looked at me. Then I caught her hurt, and just rushed in and gave her a hug. For a second she held off, then hugged me back.

'I've missed you,' she said as we drew apart.

'And that stuff about Alice?'

'Rubbish. Now tell me what you've been doing,' said Anne. From the look on her I didn't dare refuse.

And so I told her. I could see from her face it was a bit of a shocker. *The Frank Storm Story – The Facts!* I gave her the full details, how and where I did it and all that.

When I had finished she said, 'So why didn't you tell me?'

I hesitated. 'I thought . . . you might tell.'

She stamped her foot. 'Frances!'

'Sorry.'

'Sorry, sorry, sorry . . . I could strangle you!'

We were silent a little while.

'What were you doing near your house as Frank?' said Anne finally.

'Well,' I said, wanting to come as clean as possible, 'I used to just practise being Frank in my bedroom. In front of the mirror and all that. But once I'd been out as Frank, to matches and training . . . I thought why not practise him outside. So sometimes I walk about as him. Try him out on people.'

'Suppose your Mum or Dad had come out?'

'I'd have run for it.'

72

'You didn't run from me though.'

'I didn't want to,' I said.

'Hm,' she said, half-satisfied. 'Now show me what you do in the shed.'

We went in. And I showed her my bag hidden under the sacks.

'I keep my stuff here when I don't want to go around with my bag.' I held my nose. 'It's a bit musty – but there's hardly anyone over here, and when there is, they're working.' Then I remembered. 'Except the first time. Dad nearly caught me. Chased me all over the plots. If he'd have got me, he'd have chucked me in the water tank.'

Anne was looking over Dad's tools and pots. Just under them was a bucket of brown liquid and a length of hose, and by it a bottle of Bovril and a packet of sugar.

'Hey,' I said, 'wanna see Dad's marrow?'

'Yes,' said Anne. 'Let's see the famous marrow.'

I locked up the shed, and took Anne round the path on to the plot. We went through the tomatoes, and just past the patch of corn. There it lay, held up by planks and sticks. Like a fat sow in a nest of straw.

'Your dad grew that?' said Anne in a hushed voice.

It did look even bigger today, seeing it with Anne. I'd sort of got used to it over the summer.

'He only grows one,' I said. 'He takes off all the little ones, so all the fertilizer and stuff just goes into that one. He goes up to London Zoo to buy elephant manure. Half a tonne for just one marrow.'

'Is he going to eat it?' said Anne.

I laughed. ''Course not. It'd taste horrible. Little ones are nicest. No – he's going to put it in the Allotment Show. He came second last year in the biggest marrow section, and this year he swears he'll win. It's so much bigger than his last one.'

Anne knelt down and tried to put her arms round it, and couldn't.

'He wants it to be 150 centimetres round,' I said.

Anne couldn't take her eyes off it. 'It's like a barrel,' she said. 'Though I can't see much point in it if you don't eat it.'

'You'd be eating it for a year,' I said, and grimaced. I can't stand marrow anyway. It just seems like mush to me.

'He's doing something funny to it,' I said. 'I saw him when he caught me in the shed. Look.'

I had spotted two clothes pegs on the ground. I searched the marrow skin until I found a crack. I pushed and pulled until I managed to get a finger in, then I pushed a peg in with the other hand. I moved the peg sideways and forced the other one in.

'That's what he does,' I said. 'Then he's got some liquid he pours in. Bovril and sugar I think.' I turned to the shed where I'd seen the bucket of brown liquid.

'What's happening?' called Anne.

I turned back to the marrow. Brown liquid was gurgling out of the hole. The hole was compressing in and out like two fat lips. By the time I realized what was happening and took out the clothes pegs, it was too late. The liquid continued pouring out, like it had been pumped in all summer and had just had enough.

I tried squeezing the hole shut, I tried sitting on the marrow, but out it came. The marrow had just had enough of being pumped full. After about two minutes, the marrow lay flat on the ground like a burst inner tube.

'Crikey,' I exclaimed. 'Dad'll go crazy. We'd better clear off. Sharpish.'

'Too late,' said Anne.

She pointed to the allotment gate. There was Dad coming through, whistling 'The Skye Boat Song'.

19

I pulled Anne gently back behind the shed, where we crouched down and watched Dad.

As he was coming, he spotted someone he knew who was digging part of his plot. Dad stopped to talk. The man offered Dad some runner beans. They continued chatting for a while.

'We've got to get away,' I said.

'We can't,' said Anne. 'Not with them there.'

We watched them talking. They say women can talk, but my Dad can certainly natter. Football, allotments, boxing – you just have to stand him up and pull the string.

'Can't you just explain?' said Anne.

I looked at her. She just didn't understand about Dad and his marrow. 'Every spare minute he's had this summer he's been working on it,' I said. 'We couldn't go on holiday because of it. My mum says he loves it more than he loves his family. He wraps it up, unwraps it, waters it leaf by leaf . . .'

Anne said quietly, 'Is he all alright?'

'I sometimes wonder,' I said.

'Your whole family . . .' she began.

'What?'

'Well, if it isn't football, football, football, it's marrows, marrows, marrows . . .'

'Or dolls' houses, dolls' houses, dolls' houses.'

'You're a bunch of loonies,' she said.

I thought about that for a second. Maybe we were. We let

things take us over. We ate them, dreamt them, slept them. What seemed really important to us made other people think we were crazy.

'He wants the World Champion Marrow,' I said.

'What for?'

'Everyone wants to be able to do something well.'

She looked to where he was still talking, and then whispered, 'But wasn't he cheating?'

I nodded. He was; I had seen him.

'What's the point of that?' asked Anne.

I didn't say anything. But I knew why he wanted to do it. He wanted to be seen as the best. He wanted to be in the *Guinness Book of Records*. He wanted to be noticed.

Then he was coming over, the runner beans over his shoulder. He made his way through the tomato plants, past the corn . . .

I ran out. 'Dad!'

He didn't seem to hear me. I ran across the allotment to him, where he was standing by his marrow plant. His hands were held against his jaw, gazing in disbelief at the collapsed marrow. Then his body seemed to collapse, too. He was on his knees on the ground, his hands covering his face. I didn't know what to say.

'My marrow,' he moaned. 'My beautiful marrow.'

I put my hand on his shoulder. 'Dad . . .'

He turned to look at me. 'Look what they done,' he said. 'Look what they done to my champion.'

In his hands, the skin of the marrow was lying like a dead body. The dead body of his dreams. He wasn't famous, my dad. He wasn't the man who grew the world's biggest marrow. He was just a taxi driver, an ordinary taxi driver, who dripped Bovril and sugar into a marrow.

I said, 'I did it, Dad.'

I felt a charge go through his body, and I thought, *He's going to hit me; he's going to strike me dead.* But he didn't move.

'I was just showing Anne where you poured the brown liquid in, when it all came running out.'

Anne had now joined us. 'That's all she did, Mr Fairweather,' she said.

In a weak voice Dad said, 'How did you know about the brown liquid?'

'I saw you,' I said.

Dad rose, and took a handkerchief from his pocket and wiped his eyes.

'I saw you with the tubing and funnel,' I continued. 'And the bucket of stuff . . .'

Dad kicked the marrow. It squelched liquid, splashing his foot. 'You know what I've been doing?' he said.

I nodded.

'I've been doing it all summer,' he muttered, 'and what for, you may well ask.'

He turned to face me, still tears in his eyes. This wasn't a man who was going to shout at me. This wasn't a man about to beat the living daylights out of me. This was just my Dad, and he was as empty as his marrow. 'I've been cheating,' he said quietly.

I looked to Anne; she put a finger to her lips.

'I thought by cheating I could *be* someone.'

Then he straightened up, looking down at that poor heap of a marrow. 'All I put into *that*. The sweat . . . the love . . . And for what?'

He marched over to his compost heap where his wheelbarrow lay upside down. He picked up the barrow and wheeled it back. 'I'm glad it's over,' he said.

He loaded the collapsed marrow into the wheelbarrow, and threw in the leaves and stalks.

77

'It's one thing making a fool of myself. That's bad enough,' he said as he barrowed it over to the compost heap. 'It would have been quite another thing making a disgrace of myself.'

He threw the marrow on the heap.

'Thanks, Frances,' he said. 'You saved me from that.'

20

The next day in school, late afternoon, I was drawing and labelling a Tudor theatre.

It was an outdoor theatre, circular with balconies. I wondered if you could play five-a-side football in it. Then it struck me that maybe they did. Between shows. It wasn't a bad space for a kick-about.

Ms Natches was looking over my shoulder. 'Quite good, Frances. Definitely an improvement.'

I smiled at her. She wasn't all that bad. Sometimes.

'I want to speak to you and Anne after school.'

I looked up at her.

'It's all right,' she said. 'This is not a telling-off. It's good news.'

She didn't say any more. And I thought, *I bet she's going to let me off my ban with the Perils.* A little later I glanced over to Anne. She gave me a thumbs-up sign. So Anne thought so, too. I crossed my fingers. Maybe today was going to be it. The end of my banning. I crossed my legs, and even crossed my eyes. I double-dared hoped so. It would be so good to play football with my friends again.

The rest of the afternoon seemed to drag along after that. I kept looking at the clock, but the hands were weighted down. I got so desperate in the end that I even read about Tudor theatres, but there wasn't any mention of football.

At last the day ended, and I waited behind with Anne. Then, to my surprise, Dad showed up. He poked his head

79

nervously round the classroom door. Ms Natches was having a word with another parent.

'Be with you in a minute,' she said.

'Right,' he answered, and came in.

'Hello, Dad,' I said. I was sitting on a table. Anne was playing with the class guinea pig.

'Your teacher phoned me at lunchtime.'

'About what?'

'She said there's been some improvement,' said Dad. 'Your work's getting better. And more surprising, there's less cheek.'

I looked at him wide-eyed. 'Me? Cheeky?'

Dad nodded. 'And *I've* noticed an improvement as well.'

I smiled at him slyly. 'Getting more ladylike, eh, Dad?'

'I wouldn't go quite that far. I wondered whether all that football was making you too aggressive.'

What was this leading up to? I waited. He sat on the table by me.

'So why,' he said, 'do you think there's been an improvement in your behaviour since you stopped playing?'

I didn't answer. I didn't want to answer. After all, I couldn't say to him that I'd been playing all along – for the Tigers. Luckily Ms Natches interrupted us, as the other parent left.

'Sorry I kept you waiting, Mr Fairweather.'

'We've been having a chat,' he said.

'Come and join us, Anne. I've got some news.'

'Can I bring Tingle?' she asked.

Ms Natches nodded, and Anne came across cuddling the guinea pig. I gave it a stroke. He's so soft and he has these big brown eyes.

'Now keep calm,' said Ms Natches. 'I've got a surprise.'

We all looked to her.

'Don't hold out on us,' said Dad.

'I've got another match for the Perils,' she said.

'Oh, well done, Ms Natches!' exclaimed Anne, nearly dropping Tingle. She paused for an instant, bit her lip and said, 'I want Frances to play.'

I looked at the floor. 'That's not up to me.'

'Please, Mr Fairweather, Ms Natches. She's our best player, and we've got injury problems . . .'

'What do you think?' said Dad to Ms Natches.

She pursed her lips. 'I don't know. I mean her work has improved a bit, but it might just backslide . . .'

Anne pipped in, 'I'll make sure she keeps up her school-work.'

I thought, *Whose side is she on?*

After a pause Ms Natches said, 'All right. I'm probably making a huge mistake, but you can play. That's . . . if your father agrees.'

We all turned to Dad.

Dad said, 'She's got me out of a lot of trouble recently, so I can't say no.'

I gave Dad a cuddle. 'Oh, thanks, Dad!'

'Thanks, Mr Fairweather,' said Anne. 'Thanks, Ms Natches.'

'Thanks, Ms Natches,' I said. 'You won't regret it. I promise to work . . .'

'Don't promise too hard, love,' laughed Dad.

I threw my arms up in the air. I was free again. 'Hooray – the ban's off! I can play for the Perils! Eeaiadeo! We got a match!'

'Calm down, calm down,' said Dad, putting an arm on my shoulder.

I turned to Anne and gave her a hug. 'I'm so glad to have a game with the girls again.'

Anne said, 'I'm going to arrange extra training sessions, and anyone who doesn't come is out of the team.'

'So who's it with?' said Dad.

Ms Natches smiled coyly. 'Wouldn't you like to know.'

'West Ham United?' joked Anne.

Ms Natches gave half a nod. 'Well, you're on the right lines . . .'

I began to get worried. 'What do you mean?'

'Well, it's not a girls' team,' said Teacher.

'Who then?' said Dad.

'It's with the Tigers,' said Ms Natches.

'The Tigers!' I exclaimed. My head was working overtime. 'When is it?'

'Saturday,' said Ms Natches. 'Kick-off at three. Wanstead Flats.'

Dad said, 'I'll see if I can get along.'

But for me, the world had turned upside down. I had *already* promised to play for the Tigers on Saturday.

'Apparently,' said Ms Natches, 'they've got a new striker who is supposed to be brilliant. But I think our Frances might show him a thing or two.'

I can't play for both sides, I thought.

'Ms Natches,' I began, nervously. 'I've been thinking – maybe I shouldn't play . . . I mean they're good. I'm out of practice.'

'Nonsense,' she said. 'This is your chance to show that creep. He's a real show-off they say. Frank something or other. This is your chance to show him what we're made of.'

Anne was looking at me carefully. I could see she had realized.

'Well, it's difficult,' I said. 'I mean I *do* get obsessed with football. Maybe you and Dad are right.'

Dad put his arm round my shoulder. 'It's all right,

Frances. I've said you can play and I mean it. We both agree, don't we, Ms Natches?'

'We do,' she said.

'But football is bad for me,' I pleaded. 'It makes me aggressive and cheeky. I'll neglect my schoolwork . . .'

Ms Natches sighed. 'We've been through all that.'

I was desperately thinking, *I must get out of this match. I've already promised the Tigers. I can't play for both sides*.

'I can see her point,' said Anne. Good old Anne. 'Maybe we should give Frances another week or two to straighten out.'

'I'm surprised at you, Anne,' said Ms Natches. 'After that petition you gave me . . .'

Anne looked glum.

'Frances has been very good this week,' said Dad. 'The way she helped me out the other day, she deserves this chance.'

'But, Dad . . .' I was clean out of reasons.

'Enough, Frances,' said Ms Natches. 'We all know you love football. So, unless you've got some other reason . . .'

'Course not,' said Dad. 'What could *that* be?'

'I've no idea, Mr Fairweather, but I would have expected her to jump at the chance.'

'Don't you want to play, love?' said Dad.

How could I tell him I didn't? How could I tell him I was already playing? But for another team.

'Now don't muck us about, Frances,' said Ms Natches. 'Are you in or out?'

'I'm playing, of course,' I exclaimed. 'Can't anyone take a joke?'

'It wasn't very funny,' said Ms Natches.

'Strange sense of humour my daughter,' said Dad. 'Must run in the family. Anyway, now that's sorted, I'm off to pick your mum up with a dolls' house she's repairing. Don't be late for tea.'

Dad left, and Ms Natches saw him to the door.

'What you going to do, Frances?' whispered Anne.

'If I'm playing for the Perils,' I said, 'I'd better make sure I'm not playing for the Tigers.'

'How will you do that?'

'There's a training session this evening,' I said. 'Sh!'

Dad had gone and Ms Natches was coming back to join us.

'Well, Frances. I'm really looking forward to this match. If we all sharpen up during the week . . . eh?'

'Yes,' I said.

'Are you worried about it? I know their striker's good . . . Frank Big Boots. But I think you're better.'

'Thank you,' I said.

'No, I mean it,' said Ms Natches. 'I think in a tackle you'll take the ball from anyone. And I bet you're faster. Don't worry about Frank thingumabob. Once you stand up to him, you won't have any trouble.'

I nodded weakly.

Teacher continued, 'Anne and I will organize some extra training. And then we just go for it. All right – you're a bit rusty. The worst that can happen is we'll lose. But I think we might give those boys rather a surprise.'

21

I had agreed to play for the Perils. That was definite. So I could not play for the Tigers. That, too, was definite. There is, after all, only one of me – no matter what it may seem.

I went to the training session at the Tigers' ground after school. I decided to talk to Stan as soon as I got a chance. I was a bit late for the session as there were people over the allotment, and I didn't want to be seen going into the shed, so I had to hang around a little while.

When I got there, training had started, and Stan ushered me out on the field. It was windy and chilly: the sort of weather that makes you think winter will come early. The first leaf-falls were gusting on the pitch.

The team were doing passing practice in squares. Then we switched to practice in trapping the ball. We did this in pairs. One threw in a high ball, the other had to stop the ball dead. Stan ran around, his usual self, complaining and cajoling, and sometimes joining in to show someone how they *should* be doing it.

After some time he called a halt, and beckoned everyone over to the hut. He got us all sitting down, and then got Cliff to hand round the juice. This was usual the training session before a match day. Stan would talk tactics, and try to get us in fighting mood. I thought, *Once he's had his blab I'll tell him I can't play Saturday*. He wasn't going to like it but I'd just have to face that.

He got us to sit round in a half-circle facing him. We were well-warmed up, and the shed was a windbreak. Stan was holding a newspaper, and was looking even more excited than usual.

'Can we have a bit of hush, team,' he said. 'You 'n' all, John.'

We all pulled in for the lecture, finishing off our orange juice.

'Now, about Saturday,' began Stan, like a teacher of infants at story time. 'You're probably wondering why I fixed up a match with the Perils.'

I was past wondering.

'A girls' team,' he went on. 'Especially as my attitude to girls and football is well-known.'

I might've laughed at this, if I didn't have other things on my mind.

'So, look at this,' said Stan and unwrapped his newspaper.

There was a whole page of girl players. Photos of teams, and some individual shots. The main photo was a girl in front of the goal, with two defenders coming for her. I looked at it again. Crikey – it was me! Frances, I mean. I remembered that shot. It was from about six weeks ago against Shaftesbury School, and I had scored.

'A whole page of girl players,' said Stan, glaring at us, daring us to say anything. 'The borough sports department is encouraging girls to play football. Encouraging! Well I want the Tigers to do a little *dis*couraging. Football is a male game. Invented by men for men. Don't get me wrong, I like girls: as supporters, cheer-leaders, and so forth. But respecting the maleness of the sport. So, I expect you to beat the Perils, as they call themselves, double figures – and show once and for all who this game is for. The rest of this week we are going to concentrate on tactics, something a girls' team will know little about.' He rolled up the paper. 'Any questions?'

Alec called out. 'I hear they've got an ace striker.'

Stan smiled. 'You frightened, Alec?'

'No, just, you know...'

'Sure, I know,' said Stan. 'That's why we've got to plan tactics. We won't give her an inch. Hassle her, crowd her. Don't give her any room. And get those balls up front for our own ace striker. Eh, Frank?'

I didn't say anything. I was going to have to tell him that his ace striker wouldn't be there. Or not playing for the Tigers, at any rate.

'We keep pushing forward,' he went on. 'Keep the ball in their half, long passes – that way their strikers will die of cold.' He paused a second. 'So, OK – let's get back out there. Groups of three. Let me see those long passes.'

The team got up, put their cups on the tray and went out to the pitch. Except for me. I waited until all the rest were out of earshot.

'Stan,' I said. 'I got a problem.'

He turned to me, all smiles. 'What's that, Frank?'

'I can't play Saturday.'

His face turned blue. His jaw dropped. For a few seconds he was fighting for words. 'Against the Perils! Frank, you must. I need you.'

I played it cool, though my stomach felt it was full of bees. 'Sure I want to, Stan. But well . . .' I thought quick. I needed something good. 'It's my sister's wedding.'

'I didn't know you had a sister.'

'Oh, I do. And she's getting married. I'm a page.'

Stan clapped his hands on his ears. 'This is terrible news.'

'Yeah,' I said trying to look really sorry. 'I so much wanted to play, but you know . . .'

Eyes to the sky, he strode around as if in terrible pain. 'I don't believe it. I just don't believe it.'

'Sorry, Stan. I would if I could. But a sister is a sister . . .'

Stan stopped and put a hand to his chin. 'Where's the wedding?'

'Er . . . local church.'

'What time?'

'Er . . . three thirty.'

'Pity,' he sighed. 'The match starts at three.'

I felt better. His questions were coming too quick. I hadn't thought it all out, and I could have been in trouble.

'Hell, Frank,' he appealed to me. 'You're the best striker I've got. All my plans involve you.'

'I would if I could,' I said regretfully, 'but you can't cancel a wedding – can you?'

Stan snapped his fingers. 'But you can cancel a football match!'

'I don't get you.'

He turned to me, eyes alight. 'Maybe we can switch the game to the morning.'

'I'm not even sure about the morning,' I said in alarm. 'I've got to bath, wash my hair, get dressed. For the wedding.'

'You could make it, Frank.'

'No,' I said. 'It's not on. I've just too much to do.'

He slapped his wristwatch. 'Suppose I got a ten o'clock kick-off? Sixty minutes play, ten minutes at half-time. You'll be done by half-eleven. If I send you home in a taxi, you'll have three and a half hours to get ready for the wedding.'

I was beginning to panic. This wasn't going right at all.

'Don't change the match time just for me,' I said. 'It's not fair on everyone else.'

'Don't worry about that, boy. We need you. I'll phone their manager. See if she agrees.'

'But it's not fair,' I said in despair.

'Why not, if she agrees?' Then he looked at me close.

88

Maybe he had picked up on the way I had said it. 'Don't you want to play, Frank?'

''Course I do,' I said. 'But . . .' I had run out of buts.

'Then I'll phone,' said Stan.

With that, he turned away, and strode round the pitch. His shoulders rounded, a determined bear of a man. He was off to the phone box just outside the park. I wanted to run after him and pull him back. I wanted to jump the fence and wreck the phone.

I gripped my fists, digging my nails into my palms. My last hope was Ms Natches. 'Come on, Hatchback. Turn him down. Tell him where he can get off.' With any luck she'd be fixed up for the morning, visiting her old granny in hospital or something . . . If I had had a lucky penny, I would have spun it. If I had had a rabbit's paw I would have rubbed it. I'd have gripped my horseshoe and sworn by my black cat.

I couldn't play for both sides.

I saw him coming back through the gates. Maybe she wasn't in. Maybe the phone was vandalized.

He swung his arms high in the air, then cupped his hands round his mouth. 'It's all right!' he hollered. 'She's agreed.'

22

I sprinted over to the allotment. Dad was pulling up plants that had finished, and was throwing them on his wheel-barrow. The shed was open and I got changed at top speed. I sneaked in and out without being seen.

At least I was Frances again, even if I *was* in a mess. I had now agreed to play for both teams. Stan had changed the time of the match for me, and Ms Natches had done me a big favour by stopping my ban. Why did people have to be so helpful!

When I got near home I made an effort to look cheerful. It would be no good coming in looking like I'd just lost my life savings.

In the kitchen, Mum was tiling her roof. She had the wood on the kitchen table, plus her glue and a pile of miniature tiles.

'Hand me that spirit level,' she called as I came in. 'I don't want to let go of this row of tiles.'

I handed it over. She put it in her mouth, then switched hands with the row of tiles. Taking the spirit level from her mouth, she placed it against the lowest row on the roof she was working on.

'Damn it. Excuse my French. It's wonky.'

'Looks all right to me,' I said.

She shook her head. 'By the time I get to the eaves, one half will be over the edge.' She sat down. 'I've had enough. Nothing's gone right today.'

I knew the feeling.

There weren't any signs of dinner. I wondered whether to ask, or whether to starve to death, and so solve all my problems.

'Dolls' house for tea?' I said.

'Stuffed with marrow,' she said. 'Followed by window salad, with of course . . .'

I knew. 'Window dressing?'

Mum nodded, and began pushing all her bits and pieces aside.

I said, 'Why do you make dolls' houses, Mum?'

She sat down and wiped sawdust off her forehead. 'Most of the world, I can't do anything about. I like one bit I'm in total control of. One bit where I can be God. Put things here, people there, without any arguments. Except today, when I can't do anything right and I feel rotten.'

I felt rotten too, but I didn't want to say so, or she'd ask me why. So I said, 'Let's go out for a meal.'

Mum looked at me, looked at the mess on the table, and said, 'Why not?'

So we had a quick wash, and left a note on the table for Dad, saying where we had gone.

To the local café. It's cheap and bright, and the food isn't bad. We both ordered, and when the food came I found I couldn't eat. I didn't want to eat.

Mum was chomping away busily, and didn't notice me for a while. 'Your father,' she said, 'hasn't mentioned his marrow for two days. Two whole days. I wonder what's happened.'

'I'm sorry, Mum,' I said pushing my plate away. 'I'm just not hungry.'

'Not even the egg or the sausage . . . ?'

I shook my head. I felt like crying.

'What's wrong, lovey?'

91

She put a hand to my face. My mum's got big strong hands; gentle hands.

'Nothing,' I said.

'Nothing, sweetheart? It doesn't look like nothing to me.'

And I *would* have told her, but Dad came in then. He was annoyed we hadn't waited for him, so we had a quiet row in the cafe. Neither of them wanted to shout, so they hissed at each other across the table.

'You knew I'd be back by seven.'

'No, I didn't.'

'Yes, you did, I told you.'

'When?'

After that, I stopped listening. It became like background music. There – but you don't have to listen to it. I wondered if I could go sick on Saturday. Send Ms Natches or Stan a note, I hadn't decided which. But then Ms Natches would just phone up Mum and Dad, and I couldn't believe Stan would just accept a note. He'd find out where I lived from whoever gave him the note, and he'd be round by jet plane.

'To change the subject,' I heard Mum say. 'What's happened to your marrow?'

I glanced up. Dad was gazing intently at a piece of meat on his plate. 'Virus attack,' he said. 'Dead sudden.'

'But it was huge,' Mum said.

'One minute it was,' he said, 'and the next, well . . .' He turned to me. 'You saw it, didn't you, Frances?'

I nodded. 'Like a burst beach-ball,' I said. 'Virus, was it then, Dad?'

Dad shifted uncomfortably. 'Yes, virus.'

'The marrow was like an airship,' I said, 'and then it just seemed to pop.'

Dad was staring at me. Mum put a finger to her lips. I got the hint. She knew something wasn't quite right, but didn't want to know. And Dad didn't want any more jokes at his expense.

'It was awful,' I said.

'Poor Ron,' said Mum, putting her hand over his.

'Serves me right,' said Dad, 'for putting so much work into it.'

They held hands on the tablecloth.

Mum sighed. 'I'm going to have to start again on the roof.'

'I thought you'd nearly finished it,' said Dad.

'So did I,' said Mum, 'but I lined the tiles up wrong.'

'Can't you just take them off?'

She pursed her lips. 'That glue is stronger than the wood itself.'

'Poor Lil,' said Dad. He gave her fingers a squeeze.

'And poor Frances,' said Mum.

'What's up with her?' said Dad.

'I just feel a bit miserable,' I said.

So we had a three-way squeeze, and I felt a bit better. After all, it wasn't Saturday *yet* . . . and I wasn't the only one with problems.

Dad ate my main course, and I managed to keep down the rhubarb crumble. Whoever I was playing for, I needed to keep my strength up.

23

On Friday after school, Ms Natches and me, as team captain, arranged a meeting for the Perils in our classroom. Not a training session – that was pointless with the match tomorrow – more a pep talk. Everyone showed up, which made a change.

I had come early and taken down enough chairs for the team. They all get stacked on the tables after school finishes. Then I'd written up the team positions on the blackboard. Everybody already knew their own, but I wanted them to see what the whole team looked like:

In goal:		Maisie	
Defenders:	Anne	Brenda	Moneeza
Midfield:		Liz Joan Puja	
Attack:	Alice	Frances Jill	Tammy

Ms Natches told us that the time of the Saturday match had been changed.

'Frank Storm, their striker, couldn't make the afternoon,' she said.

'Playing for Tottenham Hotspur, is he?' asked Liz, with a sneer.

'He scored two goals last week,' said Alice. 'My dad saw him.'

'Oh gawd!' said Maisie. She's our goalkeeper, and I know the feeling, because I've filled in when she's been off sick. If the team plays badly, being goalie is like being a punch-bag.

I noticed Frances wasn't joining in. She'd told me at

playtime that she couldn't get out of playing for the Tigers, and didn't know how to get out of playing for the Perils either.

Of *course* I wanted Frances to play for us. But it wouldn't help *me* saying so.

'I just want to say a few words about tomorrow's game,' said Ms Natches. We had arranged this beforehand. She would say her bit, then I would say my piece as captain.

'It won't be like your usual game,' she began. 'I think the boys might try to rough you out of the game. They'll try to get you scared so that you'll back off instead of going in for the tackle. And if they succeed, then they'll beat you – . But there's no reason at all why you should be scared. Girls your age are just as strong as boys – so stand up to them.'

'I think we can give as good as we get,' said Puja. And everyone joined in on that. If the Tigers tried to push us around, they'd find themselves getting pushed back.

Now it was my turn. 'But it's no good simply roughing it,' I said. 'We might as well be a team of wrestlers for that. And they're probably better at it than we are. We've got to play as a team. Play the moves we've been practising. Don't try to run forty metres with the ball. Look for your team-mates. Be in position, beat your markers. And don't let them frighten you.'

Then everyone had something to say. I can't say it added up to much, but it left us with a good team feeling. And that's about all you can do the session before a match. It's too late to do any more training, and you'd be daft planning new tactics because they just wouldn't work. All you can do is make the best of what you've got.

'Get a good night's sleep,' said Ms Natches. 'And don't worry. We're the underdogs. Everyone expects us to lose. They've got all the worries, 'cos we just might beat'em.'

That raised a cheer, which was a great way to end.

I left school with Frances. We'd hung back a bit in the playground because she didn't want to talk to the others. They'd sensed something wasn't quite right and left us to it. We stopped by the wall on the corner of her street. It's our regular chatting spot, under the lamp.

'What am I going to do?' she said.

She sat on the wall, kicking her legs, looking for answers in the pavement. A tree behind the wall hung over her with bright-red berries, its leaves turning yellow and red.

'I suppose,' I said, 'you could chop yourself down the middle. One arm and one leg for each side.'

'If I play for the Tigers, the Perils'll be a player short . . . If I play for the Perils, then the Tigers'll be a player short.'

'And whoever you let down will murder you.'

'What if I made up a note in blood, saying Frances and Frank have been kidnapped . . .'

'Why would anyone want to kidnap them?'

She looked at me appealingly. 'To put them into meat pies?'

'Oh, *very* likely.'

'It was fun at first. All that rough stuff being Frank. Teasing half the world. Taking the mickey out of Stan. And when I got fed up with it, I could be me again. I fooled them completely.'

'You were brilliant, Frances.'

'*Too* brilliant.' She stopped talking for a little while, and seemed to bunch up into a ball on the wall, her head in her hands. I'd never heard her so miserable. 'Maybe Frances should disappear. I should go somewhere where nobody knows me, and be Frank all the time.'

'But Frank is a game.'

'So's Frances. She's just a game I play better, because

I've been playing her longer. I could be Frank if I wanted.'

'Not once you grew up you couldn't.'

'I don't want to grow up and be a secretary.'

'So what *do* you want to be, then?'

'I don't want to be messed about with this boy–girl stuff. I don't want people saying you can't do this, that or the other because you wear a dress sometimes.'

'Oh come on – you're not doing so bad.'

'Would they ban a boy from playing football? I bet they wouldn't.'

I gave up arguing. Frances was in an awful mood. Maybe she'd picked up a bit of Frank. But I couldn't understand what she was saying when she said Frances was a game. A game has rules. Do we have rules? Do we have a dice and dice box?

'What is a boy?' said Frances. 'What is a girl? When is a girl not a girl? When is a boy not a boy?'

The answers to these questions seemed so obvious to me that I didn't answer. Everyone knows what a boy is. Everyone knows what a girl is. I couldn't understand why anyone would ask the question.

'Boy girl, boy girl, boy girl . . .' Frances began saying over and over. 'What would happen if you brought up a boy as a girl?'

'*I* don't know,' I said.

'What would happen if you brought up a girl as a boy? What would she be?'

'Forget this stuff, Frances,' I said, feeling a little frightened for her. 'And you'd better stop being Frank. Or you won't know *what* you are.'

'Boy girl, boy girl, boy girl, boy girl,' Frances went on over and over.

'Say something else,' I exclaimed.

97

'Girl boy, girl boy, girl boy . . .'

I sighed. 'I'll go home . . .'

'Boy girl.'

'What are you going to do about the match?'

'Girl boy.'

'Please, Frances, answer me sensibly.'

She lifted up her head and looked at me. 'I'm going to play,' she said.

'Who for?'

'Boy girl,' she said.

I left her sitting on the wall.

24

On Saturday morning at 9.40 I walked over to Wanstead Flats with Mum and Dad. I had got changed at home and put a tracksuit on top. I made sure it was the new one, and not the one I used for Tigers training sessions.

I was jittery and hadn't had much breakfast. Just a bowl of cereal and some juice. There were too many other things on my mind for me to bother about food.

It was a warm morning, warmer than I like it for football, and the sun was sweeping up the last of the mist as we came to the changing rooms. Ms Natches was there in her blue tracksuit. She saw me and ticked me off on the clipboard she was carrying.

'Good. That's everyone,' she said.

Mum and Dad went to have a chat with her and I went into the Ladies' changing room. I dumped my bag, said hello to Liz and Puja who were getting changed, and went off to the loo. When I'd finished there I went back outside.

And saw Stan outside the men's changing room. He wasn't looking happy, and I knew why.

One of his players hadn't shown up.

I kept my distance, and took care not to catch his eye. Every so often he would look at his watch and sigh. I left him shouting for Cliff and John. *There's more shouting to come*, I thought.

Our pitch was close by and I could see the girls kicking about round one of the goals, and the boys round the other. I jogged over, and, as I came up, Anne left the others and ran up to greet me.

'Atta girl!' she said slapping my hand. 'I knew you'd go for us.'

I put on a smile.

'Good turnout,' said Anne.

Around the pitch were maybe a hundred people; quite a few mums and dads whom I recognized and a group of girls from school. They were wearing bobble hats and scarves in the blue and white Perils colours. Anne gave them a wave, and I thought I'd better, too; that set them off on the Perils chant:

We follow the Perils
We're the only team
You'll get the leavin's
The Perils take the cream

It's the big match
It's the great match
It's the match of the year!

Oh yes, I thought, as I waved. *It'll be the match of the year all right. But not the one you're expecting.*

A group of boys on the other side of the pitch were wearing orange-and-black scarves and hats; the Tigers' colours. Tigers didn't have a song, but I could see one of the boys trying to make up for it. He was working furiously with a scrappy bit of paper and a pencil, and in a little while they gave us their chant:

We follow the Tigers
We know we're the best
We'll lick you hollow
We'll pass any test

It's the big match

It's the great match
It's the match of the year!

Not a song for Stan, I thought. *He's got other things on his mind.*

I began jogging around, and joined the girls, who were all excited. I didn't have much to say and concentrated on warming up. I did some arm-swinging and toe-touching, then got a football and did a few toe and knee bounces which set our supporters off chanting again.

Inside, I was as tense as a spring, wondering just when the bomb was going to go off. And who'd go up in the explosion.

The referee came on the pitch; a small man, with a pink face, dressed in black shorts and black shirt with white collar and cuffs. He had a watch and whistle round his neck.

I could see it was near time, so I took my tracksuit off and left it with Ms Natches, who was with Mum and Dad on the sideline.

'You show 'em,' said Dad.

'Just don't panic, Frances,' said Ms Natches, 'and stick to the plan.'

I ran back on the pitch, thinking, *What plan – hers or mine?*

The ref gave two sharp blows on his whistle and waved us into position. I ran up to the centre line, and could see, if I hadn't known already, that my opposite number wasn't there.

Stan was on the pitch speaking to the ref. Ms Natches was called over. I could hear them clear enough as it was all going on a few metres from where I was positioned.

Stan told them that one of his boys hadn't shown up.

Ms Natches said, 'To make it fair then, we'll play with ten players.'

Stan shook his head. 'No. It's up to us to turn up with a full team.'

'But in the circumstances . . .' began Ms Natches.

'It's our problem,' he said firmly. 'Not yours. I'll see if I can get a substitute.'

'Then let's delay kick-off for quarter of an hour.'

'No,' said Stan. 'A ten o'clock kick-off is a ten o'clock kick-off.'

Ms Natches tried but Stan just refused her offers. Maybe he thought his ten could beat our eleven anyway. Maybe he just didn't want any favours from a girls' team manager.

Ms Natches said, 'Have it your way, then,' and left for the sideline. Stan went over to Cliff.

'Play defensive till I get back with a substitute. Don't take any risks.'

'Don't worry,' said his captain.

'Just wait till I get hold of Frank . . .' exclaimed Stan. 'He won't be fit to play tiddly-winks when I've done with him.'

He rushed off, steam rising.

Cliff changed his team around, pointing here and there, to try and swallow the hole in the front line, but he only left a hole somewhere else. The Tigers had problems.

The ref called Cliff and Anne for the toss. The ref spun the coin, Anne called and lost.

And play started.

From that first kick, when Cliff passed the ball back to his midfield players, the pattern was set. The whole of the Tigers were in defence, making their half so crowded that we had little room for tactics and hardly a chance at goal.

I didn't like it one bit. I was being followed everywhere, and it was hard to get anywhere near the goal. And when any of us did, we just seemed to fizzle out in a feeble shot that was either cleared by a defender or gave the goalkeeper no problem.

Play was all in the Tigers' half, occasionally spilling into the Perils' but the Tigers weren't interested in scoring goals and so didn't follow up. They just dropped back. In we would come and hit their brick-wall defence.

I suppose it was all they could do with one player down, but it was rotten to play against, and made for bad football. There was lots of wild kicking on both sides. The Tigers were just trying to clear the balls, and we were trying to get them nearer. Scrappy stuff.

The first sign of a chance came in the twelfth minute. I was calling for the ball from Alice, but instead of letting me have it, she tried a shot at goal which just sort of dripped into the goalkeeper's hands.

'Pass, pass!' I yelled at her. 'I was waiting for it!'

In the sixteenth minute, things picked up after a throw-in from Tammy. Liz got the ball and centred it, right where I wanted it. I broke away from my marker and saw a gap between the defenders. I slammed the ball left-footed.

And sent it past the post.

It can't have been more than a hand-width away. The goalie would never have been able to touch it. But there you go, a miss is a miss.

'Nice try,' yelled Alice.

'Next one!' exclaimed Puja, slapping me on the back.

'We've got 'em on the run,' called Anne.

She was right. The boys were flustered, and blamed each other for the breakthrough. Cliff was yelling and pointing backwards and forwards.

Two corner-kicks got us nowhere. There were so many Tiger players in the goal area that there was hardly room to swing a cat, let alone take a shot. Back and forth went the ball; it was more like a game of tennis than a football match.

Then Anne decided on a new tactic. She ran amongst us quietly telling us what to do. The plan was to draw the

Tigers out of position. She got the midfield to drop back to the halfway line, and our defenders back into our own half, instead of having us all in on the attack.

It was a risky tactic. If we weren't careful, the Tigers might get through and score, but what we wanted was to spread them over the field, so that when our attack got back into the Tigers' half we'd find our way clearer to the goal.

For about five minutes, the Tigers weren't tempted. Then in the twenty-third minute they had the ball and three attackers on the halfway line. Cliff decided to go for it. He passed to John, who raced down the wing.

'Cross it!' yelled Cliff just outside the box.

From the halfway line I could see Anne, our defender, closing in on John, who was in possession. She was hedging side to side between him and Cliff to stop him passing. He tried to get it past her, but his long run had obviously tired him and she drew it off his foot. She ran forward ten metres, crossed it to Puja, who slugged it into the Tigers' half.

I went racing deep into their half. Behind me I could hear Cliff screaming at his team to get back to defence. Alice lobbed one forward, and I ran on to it, just beating a defender. I backpassed to Alice, who slipped it to Jill.

I raced in to the centre, waving for it. Jill crossed it to me. I raced a defender for it, dummied him, got a glimpse of the goalkeeper and shot where he wasn't.

Goal!

That most beautiful cry. I raced back, arms aloft, and the whole team were round me hugging and cheering. For a brief minute the world was mine.

Our supporters broke into song, arms high, scarves waving:

We follow the Perils
We're the only team

You'll get the leavin's
The Perils take the cream

It's the big match
It's the great match
It's the match of the year!

At such times it is very easy to get a swollen head.

Play restarted. And the Tigers hardly knew what hit them. It was attack on attack. Wave followed wave. Only the goalkeeper saved them from Jill's blaster in the twenty-seventh minute.

'Come on! Come on! Let's *take* this game,' screamed Alice.

'Keep 'em forward!' I yelled.

In the twenty-eighth minute Puja took a ball from Anne. She was midfield and looking for some room. I raced into a space as Puja passed to Tammy on the right wing, who ran down five metres and crossed it to me. There was a defender in front so I crossed the ball to Jill. I ran into the penalty area to receive the pass just as Jill was chopped down by John.

It was real dirty play. He wasn't going for the ball, but the player. And there I was in a space . . .

The whistle went for a free kick. Alice wasn't hurt, but I was certain as you can be that I could've scored from her pass. Hard cheese. All we could do now was make the best of a free kick.

The ref had a word with John. Lot of good that did us. The Tigers set up a wall of six players in front of the goal. There was no way through that. Alice passed sideways to me. I looked for a shot but there was no room and I passed on the wing to Jill . . .

. . . For the last kick of the first half. The whistle went. It was 1–0 to the Perils and there were thirty minutes left to play.

25

The instant the half-time whistle went, I sprinted off the field, keeping on the other side of the pitch, away from Mum, Dad and Ms Natches. I dashed into the Ladies' changing room, grabbed my bag and went straight to the toilet.

There was no one in it, which had been the reason for my dash. I chose the corner cubicle of three and locked myself in.

I started by taking my boots and socks off, followed by my Perils shirt and shorts. Quickly as I could I swapped it all for the Tigers gear from my bag. As I was doing this, Jill, Alice and Moneeza came in, full of the usual mid-match stuff: how tired they were, and who was playing well and who wasn't, what they thought of the other team.

I kept dead quiet.

'I thought they'd be 3–0 up by now,' exclaimed Alice from the cubicle next to mine.

'They are a player down,' retorted Jill.

'I bet they won't be after half-time,' said Alice.

As I retied my boots I thought, *They won't be, Alice, but you will*.

'Hurry up in there!' called Moneeza. 'I'm dying.'

There was a flurry of handle-pulling, water-running and door-banging, and in a minute I was alone again, sitting on the toilet seat with the shaving mirror, a bottle on the floor, sponge in my hand, wiping out my freckles. Then I worked on my eyebrows, darkening them.

Make-up done, I turned to the wig. I got out the double-sided tape and pulled a length off the roll, and found, to my horror, there was only ten centimetres left. I had been using it as if it would last for ever. It just looked that much bigger on the roll.

I stopped with a sudden pain below my ribs. *Why don't I just back out?* I thought. *I don't have to be Frank. Not with all those people watching.* Mum, Dad, Ms Natches, Stan, the girls . . .

I didn't want to be shown up. I didn't want the whole world knowing. *Oh why, oh why, did I ever start being Frank?* Being that dreadful boy. I sunk my face in my hands. *Safe in the dark, in this little box – why go out there and be eaten alive?*

Because *he* said so.

Why did I have to listen? Why did he muscle Frances out and take me over? *I* used to decide. I used to say when I would be him. Now *he* was saying what was what.

Hunched on the toilet seat, two voices argued; one quiet and pleading, the other loud and tough. Frances wanted to be fair, and to be fair she couldn't be Frances. Stupid girl! And Frank wanted to be Frank. Oh, he wanted to be! He wanted to be out there, showing them, kicking mud on the girls.

I loathed and detested him. He made me sick to the stomach. He made me come and go like a puppet. He made me him.

The argument was over. He won, of course.

I stood up and did my drill from the feet. Frank's feet, Frank's legs, Frank's body, arms, head. *I am Frank! Frank! Frank!*

And you'd better give me room.

I finished off my change, putting what tape there was in

the front of the wig, and adjusted it in the mirror. All done. I pushed my face about, stretching it this way and that. I rolled my neck and shoulders, getting his rhythms. I stretched out my arms to the side and pressed with all my strength against the side walls, and felt them pushing back. I gritted my teeth, I threw my head back. I was Samson pushing down the temple. Pushing it down on all their heads.

No one would beat Frank Storm.

I relaxed and counted to ten, breathing deeply. It was time to go. To get the hell out of this ladies' loo.

I listened. And could hear no one, just water running. I picked up the bag and belted out of the cubicle. God – there was someone by a sink. I didn't stop to look but shot out the door, and in the hallway bumped into a woman in a green tracksuit.

For a second, she just looked at me mouth agape, then yelled, 'What were you doing in the ladies' loo?'

I was lost for an instant, and then the answer was obvious.

'I'm a girl,' I said.

The woman looked at me quizzically. 'You don't look it.'

I shrugged. 'Everyone says that.'

'Sorry,' said the woman, 'but you have to be careful these days.'

''S all right,' I said, and made for the entrance.

Outside I was all a-tremble thinking of Dad, Mum, Ms Natches and the girls. I took a couple of deep breaths. Calm down, calm down.

I am Frank, I thought. *Frank!*

A car drew into the car park. Stan was in it with Andy, the substitute. I thought of running off to the pitch, but then stopped. *I might as well get started here as there*, I thought.

I clenched my nails into my palms and waited for them to

get out, and then sauntered over, as cool as only Frank can be.

'I'm here,' I called. 'Your troubles are over.'

'Where the heck have you been?' yelled Stan.

'A wheel come off me skateboard.'

'I could kill you,' he screamed. 'What's the score?'

'One up to the Perils,' I said, working hard at not caring.

Stan thrust a finger in my face. 'You get out there, and you get goals. I will *not* be shown up by a bunch of schoolgirls!'

'Cool it, man,' I said, the words coming out as slow as I could make them. 'It's all in hand. We're just giving them a goal start.' I snapped my fingers. 'Now we play football. Get me?'

'I'll get you all right,' he grunted, and then turned to Andy. 'Sorry, son. How was I to know he'd show up . . .'

Andy squinted daggers at me.

'I'd love to stay and chat,' I said, 'but I got a match to win.'

I gave them a wave and jogged off. I felt them staring hard into my back, but didn't turn. I was Frank; not popular, but Frank. And I had to stay him for the next thirty minutes.

26

I couldn't see Frances anywhere. She hadn't come for her drink with the rest of the team, and she'd missed the pep talk Ms Natches had given us. I had seen her rush off to the changing room at the beginning of half-time but not since. I wondered whether she was all right.

The girls were already going into position as I jogged over to Ms Natches, who was chatting to Mr and Mrs Fairweather on the touch-line.

'Frances hasn't come out of the changing room,' I said.

Ms Natches sighed. 'All right, Anne, I'll go and get her.'

Ms Natches went off, and I went to my position on-field. It was when I got there and turned about that I knew where Frances was.

Coming on-field was Frank Storm.

For a few seconds, I was caught out. I knew, but what could I do? She had dumped us. My first thought was to go up and punch him/her on the nose. You can't just walk out on a team.

And it was all down to me. Ms Natches would search about and wouldn't find her. There was the ref coming to the centre . . . The team were all looking at me, asking.

I started moving people about. They kept questioning me. There was no point pretending. 'Frances won't be back,' I said bitterly. 'That's why. Now, no arguments.'

It set up a panic that I couldn't do anything about. I could stretch us about but I couldn't make another player.

We were in for a clobbering. How long could we hold our one-goal lead?

I looked to the centre and Frank Storm was playing the clown. 'Where you been, Frank?' someone asked him.

'Thought I'd go to me gran's,' he hollered, 'to give the girls a chance.'

He just wasn't bothered. So long as he was all right he could cause any trouble he liked.

Just like Frances.

The referee blew his whistle for play to start. We dropped straight into defence. It was the first half all over again, except now it was *us* packing *our* half.

I glanced over to Frances' Mum and Dad. They were talking urgently to Ms Natches. Well they might. Their daughter had disappeared. When I looked back a bit later I saw Ms Natches alone. I suppose Frances' parents had gone off to look for her.

She was going to get hell when they found her.

The boys hit us with everything. Frank was here, there, everywhere, waiting for his chances. They had every player in our half except the goalkeeper. It was a defender's nightmare. As soon as you cleared a ball it came back. More like ping-pong than football, and with only half a table.

After five minutes Maisie made her first save. It was a classic. She dived across the goal-mouth and took it with both hands. The crowd applauded, and we were all round her, clapping and patting her on the back. Maisie threw the ball out to me, I took it forward a few metres until Frank came for me. I thought of kicking it straight at him, but instead I belted it up to the halfway line.

It didn't stay there long, and it was back to the firing range; with us as the targets.

In the ninth minute Cliff stopped a ball in midfield. He

tore in for ten metres, Jill came for him, and he kicked the ball past her. And from nowhere, in came Frank. He blasted the ball, and it cracked into the side post.

That really shook me. The power of it. I'd been running in, but I was totally out of the picture. I couldn't believe Frances could have made a shot like that. So how could Frank?

After thirteen minutes Maisie, bless her golden gloves, again made a magnificent save. She got her fingers to what looked like a sure-fire goal, and tipped the ball round the post for a corner. What we would have done without Maisie, I can't say. She was playing the game of her life. The corner was badly handled by the Tigers and I cleared it to the halfway line.

I couldn't leave it all to the goalkeeper.

In the sixteenth minute we had a chance. I had the ball midfield and crossed it to Alice, who tore up the wing. She went into the Tigers' half with Jill and Tammy close by. It was dangerous stuff with only ten players, but my heart went with them.

I watched from the halfway line as a defender came for Alice, who was well into their half. She shot the ball between his legs. Brilliant! She ran on to it and passed to Jill. Jill passed to Tammy, who was being crowded by two defenders. Tammy tried a shot for goal, but it was obvious all the running had tired her, and the goalkeeper had no problems with her shot.

A feeble end, but that was bound to be the way, when we had to cover so much ground in our attack. If only we could hang on. That would be one in the eye for Frank Storm. Time was passing and we were, after all, still a goal up.

Frances Fairweather – who needs you?

In the nineteenth minute Cliff passed to Frank just

outside the penalty area. I came for him. He waited for me, foot on the ball.

'Come on, girl. Take it off me, then.'

'Promise you won't cry,' I snapped, and went for him.

He waited until the last instant, then flicked it past me, and ran on to it. Alice tried to take him, he swerved round and shot for goal.

It was a great shot, but an even better save. Maisie got a touch, and tipped the ball round the side of the post for a corner. Frank ran off, punching his fist into his palm and yelling with anger.

'Temper, temper,' I taunted him.

'Rabbit, rabbit!' he yelled at me. 'Go clean your 'utch!'

Cliff went to take the corner while we packed the area. Maisie was trying to push us away as she couldn't see – when Cliff lobbed it over into the mass of us.

Frank came up like a dolphin, rising out of the sea of us, and cracked the ball with his head. Straight into the top of the net.

Goal!

Oh, it was a brilliant header, I must say that. The ball came straight off Frank's head and beat us all. But that wasn't the end of it. Nor the most important bit of it. For something else came off Frank's head in the moment of that header.

His wig.

27

Frances did what she normally did when she scored. She went charging back, arms high, cheering. And in her excitement she had no idea that her wig had come off.

You can't mistake the curls of Frances' hair, and those people who knew her didn't. A buzz ran round the pitch, players and supporters pointing, 'It's Frances. Look!' Even the boys and Stan, who didn't know Frances – they'd only met her once – could see clearly that Frank wasn't Frank.

I heard Cliff say, 'It's that girl. Remember?'

I picked up the wig and ran after Frances but she was still doing her goal run, giving the thumbs-up to everyone. She must have begun to wonder why she wasn't getting it back. Why people were pointing or why Stan scowled at her . . .

It was when she ran past Ms Natches, who called out, 'Frances!' that Frances slowed up. And when Ms Natches said it a second time, she stopped and looked round. That was when I caught her.

'Frances,' I said holding up the wig. 'I'm afraid you've lost something.'

Her hands went to her head, and she felt her own hair. For a second she froze – her mouth gaping – as if caught in a photograph, catching up with the rest of us.

Then she grabbed the wig off me, straightened it as if to put it on . . . and stopped, looking around at everyone looking back at her.

'Oh no, oh no . . .' she groaned. And sank to her knees.

I put a hand on her shoulder. She stared up at me, and I

could see she was clearly Frances. Frank had disappeared like gas from a balloon.

'What am I going to do?' she pleaded.

Cliff was running over. I said, 'Play football.'

She gazed at me blankly.

I said, 'Didn't you want to play for the Tigers as a girl?'

She nodded.

'Well now's your chance.'

Cliff ran up and gave her arm a tug. 'Come on.'

She looked at him in a daze.

'I don't care who you are,' he hissed, 'but we've got a match to finish.'

Frances got up.

'Get back in position . . . or you'll have Stan over.' The boy looked embarrassed.

'Thanks,' she said, tapping him on the shoulder as she jogged off. I could see something was happening. With each step, she looked more determined. Once in position she turned round, running on the spot, without a glance to anyone.

Frances was playing for the Tigers. As Frances.

The referee had been watching, but can't have understood. His only interest was the game. The Tigers had scored and there was still ten minutes' playing time left.

He blew up for our kick-off.

I was tired myself, but it was no time for the Perils to let up now that the game was drawn. I did my best to keep the girls at it. Tightening them up, reminding them of tactics. We had to hold them off.

The next time I looked at Frances she was definitely her old self. Running, passing – and her tackling was just class. But she had an air of mischief.

What was going on?

A ball came from midfield and I found myself racing her for it. She slapped me on the back and beat me to it. And then, instead of going for goal or passing to someone who had a scoring chance, she just had fun with the ball, dribbling round three of us as if she was wrapping us in string. When she had us totally muddled, tripping over each other, and she was tiring, she passed the ball backwards, laughing.

'Frances,' I called. 'What you up to?'

'I'm free!' she yelled. 'Free!'

Then it clicked. Soon as the whistle went, she'd have hell to pay. But until then they couldn't touch her. She *was* free. Free of all that boy–girl stuff. Free of Frank. Free to play for the Tigers in the way she had wanted to play for the Tigers. As a girl. And the grown-ups were stuck behind the touch-line as if it was an electric fence . . .

Until the whistle went.

I forgave Frances everything. She was still one of us, that was as clear as could be. She was playing for us even if she did have a Tigers shirt on. After all, the score was 1–1 and she was doing her best to make it stay that way. But more than that – I loved the cheek of it. Our Frances had played for both sides. She had been a girl for the first half and then a boy for most of the second. And now she was a girl again and saying to the world, *Now you know, what you going to do about it?*

The boys didn't seem to mind. After all, they needed her, and what could they do anyway? But Stan, poor Stan by the pile of tracksuits, was in a cloud of gloom. I kept glancing over, hoping that he might see the joke of it. But it was no joke for him. Frances was breaking all his rules.

I felt sorry for him . . . in a way.

When the final whistle blew, everyone on the pitch

surrounded Frances, all yelling at once, like farmyard geese celebrating the end of Christmas. When Cliff tried to get some hush, I helped out, and others took it up till we had quiet.

Cliff held out his hand to Frances. She came over and took it, smiling.

He said, 'I know why you did it.'

'You wouldn't let me play as a girl,' she said.

'More fool us,' he said awkwardly.

Frances held up both thumbs, and the girls cheered.

A boy called out, 'You scored both goals.'

'Neat, eh?' said Frances.

'Brilliant,' he exclaimed.

Cliff said, 'You're in trouble now.'

Frances bit her lip, and looked over her shoulder. 'Yeah.'

'Not from us,' he said.

And it was then she gave him a hug. Cliff went red, but I think he liked it, because he was grinning. His team cheered, and we did the same just as Ms Natches was making her way through the throng of players.

That quietened everyone. We backed off and gave her room. For a few seconds, Ms Natches stood before Frances, eyes wide, shaking her head. The game was over. It was back to normal rules.

'I think you have a few things to tell us, Frances.'

Frances nodded, and Ms Natches led her to the execution.

28

Half an hour later, I was at home facing them all. Anne came with me so I had some support, but it was a heavy scene. Round the kitchen table there was Mum, Dad, Ms Natches and us two girls. Mum and Dad were really peeved: they'd been chasing round in Dad's taxi for the last hour trying to find me. They'd just come back to phone the police and found us waiting.

Mum said, 'Now I want to know exactly what's been going on. No lies, no tricks, just the truth.'

There was no escaping it, so I told them the lot. Anne helped out where she knew, but there was some she didn't. I went back to the beginning when I was banned from playing with the girls, and told them how I'd tried to join the Tigers as a girl and they wouldn't have me. And then I told them how I became Frank, the things I bought, and what I did at night to become him. I told them about the matches I'd played, and how strong Frank was becoming. I told them about meeting Anne. I told them all the things that led up to me deciding to play for both sides. How I couldn't let the girls down, but Frank too had to have his way. And lastly I told them about the match, and how I became Frank at half-time in the girls' toilets.

When I'd finished, there was silence for a little while. Then Ms Natches said, 'I suppose we were lucky there wasn't enough double-sided tape.' When I looked puzzled, she added, 'Or your wig wouldn't have come off.'

Dad said, 'I think we should stop your pocket money for twenty-five years.'

Mum said, 'We were searching everywhere for you.'

I looked down at my hands.

'I wouldn't mind,' said Dad, 'but we missed the whole of the second half.'

'I saw too much of it,' said Ms Natches.

'It was him,' I insisted. 'Honest.'

The adults looked at each other.

'What do you make of that?' said Mum.

'I think she made her own mess,' said Ms Natches.

'It doesn't sound like she enjoyed it, though,' said Mum.

Dad insisted there had to be some punishment. And they had different opinions about what it should be for. For Ms Natches it was letting the side down in the match. For Dad it was all the secrecy, and Mum just hated the sound of Frank.

In the end they came up with a one-game suspension and pocket money stopped for a month. That was better than I expected, so I didn't argue.

'Count yourself lucky,' said Dad, 'that the game was a draw. Or there'd be eleven kids out for your blood.'

I knew I was lucky. I had cheated on my friends, and it was nothing to do with me that it didn't work out badly. If one of those near-misses had gone in, then the losers would've camped outside the house.

'I'm really sorry,' I said to Anne.

'It's the last time you put me through that,' she said.

'You tell her, Anne,' said Mum. Then she turned to me. 'Let's get this settled ... I want a promise that that was Frank's last match.'

'I promise.'

And I meant it. I had had *more* than enough of Frank Storm.

29

On Monday I came into the kitchen after school to find Dad waiting for me.

'How was school?' he said.

I grimaced. 'A couple of girls kept calling me Frank all day.'

'Ignore 'em,' said Dad.

'It's all I can do.'

'Did it upset you?'

'Yes.'

He put an arm round my shoulder and I sniffed back a tear. It'd been horrible.

'They'll get fed up,' said Dad.

'Hope so.'

'But let's finish it here, eh? Go get his stuff.'

I went upstairs and got the bag with Frank's gear in, and we went out into the back garden. Down the end was the bare patch where Dad lit his bonfires. It was now piled with wood and a broken old chair on top. Dad poured some white spirit in the middle, lit it and backed off.

The pile caught quickly, and in a few minutes was ablaze, the wood crackling and the flame dancing in the early autumn air.

I opened the bag. The first thing I took out was the wig. I threw it on the fire. It burned rapidly in a smoky yellow flame, hissing as it melted down into bubbles of flaming jelly. I threw on the cap and the scarf. The scarf went in no time but the peak of the cap held out until it finally fell into the embers.

Then I took out the brown leather jacket with the patched sleeves. I held it out arms wide. I could see myself in the bulk of the arms. Feel the bounce and swagger of Frank in the body of the jacket.

'He was taking me over,' I said.

Dad took the jacket off me and held it high, trying to see in it what I saw.

'Sometimes I didn't seem to be acting.' I shivered. 'Burn it, burn it. I don't want any more of him.'

Dad threw the jacket on the fire.

'What about this?' asked Dad, holding up the bag.

'Get rid of him completely,' I exclaimed.

Dad tossed it on.

The jacket was burning smokily, and smelling. Me and Dad moved out of the direction of the smoke just as Anne came into the garden from the house. She was waving a letter.

'Hey Frances – I got some news.'

'What?'

'They've accepted us in the girls' league for next season!'

'Whoopee!' I grabbed her and we did a jig round the fire. We whirled round and round.

'Careful,' exclaimed Dad.

We stopped.

'Sorry, Mr Fairweather,' said Anne.

'If you want to dance, do it away from the fire. Now – what are you saying?'

Anne explained that she'd written to the league, and she'd just got a reply. 'And they said yes,' she exclaimed.

I did another Irish jig (away from the fire) finishing with a leap to the sky.

Anne said, 'That means a match a week for the girls.'

'We'd better get the team into regular training,' I said.

'We're gonna need some extra reserves.'

'So let's get a second team going.'

'Go on some courses . . .'

'Get some new kit . . .'

'Join the Women's FA . . .'

I stopped, and put an arm round Anne. 'Fancy a kick-about? Anne Harper – Ace Organizer.'

Anne threw her head back and gave me a wink. 'Sure. What are you waiting for? Frances Fairweather – Demon Striker.'

FABER CHILDREN'S CLASSICS

The Children of Green Knowe
by Lucy Boston

The River at Green Knowe
by Lucy Boston

The Big Bazoohley
by Peter Carey

Autumn Term
by Antonia Forest

The Mouse and His Child
by Russell Hoban

Charlie Lewis Plays for Time
by Gene Kemp

Meet Mary Kate and Other Stories
by Helen Morgan and Shirley Hughes

Frances Fairweather – Demon Striker!
by Derek Smith

Marianne Dreams
by Catherine Storr

The Mirror Image Ghost
by Catherine Storr

The Sam Pig Storybook
by Alison Uttley

Make Lemonade
by Virginia Euwer Wolff